A HEAP OF KILLING

ROBERT VAUGHAN

A Heap of Killing
Paperback Edition

Wolfpack Publishing
9850 S. Maryland Parkway, Suite A-5 #323
Las Vegas, Nevada 89183

wolfpackpublishing.com

Paperback ISBN 978-1-63977-598-9
eBook ISBN 978-1-63977-889-8
LCCN 2023938164

This book is dedicated to my brother,
Phillip Vaughan
I couldn't ask for a better one

A HEAP OF KILLING

1

If anyone were to ask Lucas Cain to describe himself, he would say he was a rambling man. His propensity to move around was not driven by some deep-seated, long engrained wanderlust. It was the result of a series of significant events that had a great impact on his life.

It began with the Civil War when Lucas Cain had served in the Fifth Missouri Regiment. The next in the series of occurrences was when he was taken prisoner during the Battle of Cold Harbor, and wound up spending the last ten months of the war in the infamous Andersonville Prison.

After the war he returned home to Cape Girardeau, Missouri, where he joined the police force, got married, and had the intention of living out the rest of his life peacefully, but that was not to be. Lucas's wife and child had both died during childbirth, and that had been the final thing in the series of events which left him with nothing to keep him in Cape Girardeau. As a result, Lucas' home was the hurricane deck of a horse.

His wanderings had taken him to Colorado, where a

set of circumstances reunited Lucas with Dan Lindell, an old army friend. Dan was working with the Missouri Pacific Railroad, and he recruited Lucas to come work with him. Together, they overcame outlaws and dishonest politicians who were attempting to cheat local ranchers and farmers out of their rightful gain from the western expansion of the railroad.

With their work done, Lucas and his friend were having breakfast at Waggy's when William Lightfoot, the newspaper editor, and John Forsythe, the city marshal, came into the little café. Seeing Lucas and Dan at the table, they came over to them. Both Lightfoot and Forsythe were wearing big smiles.

"The way you two stopped the stealing and the cheating of the ranchers and farmers around here, you are just about the most popular men in town," Forsythe said. "Why either one of you could be elected mayor if you wanted the job."

"And don't think Mayor Ericson doesn't know this," Lightfoot added with a chuckle.

"You can tell the mayor for both of us, that he has no worries," Lucas said. "Dan will be going back to St. Louis, and I'll be on my way as well."

"Really?" Forsythe said. "You mean I'm going to lose the best deputy I ever had?"

Lucas chuckled. "The thing you liked most about me was that you didn't have to pay me."

The marshal joined Lucas with a little laugh. "Well, there is that."

Lucas was referring to the arrangement he and Marshall Forsythe had where Lucas had the authority of a badge but received no pay, thus allowing him to collect bounties on the men he brought in.

"Sit down and join us," Dan invited.

"Don't mind if we do," Forsythe replied.

Forsythe and Lightfoot each refilled their cups of coffee as they joined Lucas and Dan at their table.

"Are you sure you won't stay, Lucas?" Forsythe asked again. "I'll bet I could come up with some sort of arrangement that would be good for you. Maybe get you a little house, or I know, bring in a thoroughbred horse from Kentucky. I know you'd like that."

"I have to say an offer like that is tempting, but it's time to go," Lucas said.

When the meal was finished, they all exchanged handshakes.

"I need to say one more goodbye," Lucas said as he moved toward a woman standing by the counter.

"Wanda, I've enjoyed knowing you," he said, "and I want you to know that I haven't had meals this good since my own mother was the cook."

"You're not leaving are you?"

"Yes, ma'am, I am."

Wanda's eyes brimmed with tears, and she opened her arms inviting him in for a hug. "It won't be the same without you. Waggy and I will miss you."

"Listen, when we get back to Robinson, why don't you come back to St. Louis with me?" Dan asked.

Lucas shook his head. "No, I'll be going the other way."

"Where will you go?"

"You know better than to ask that."

"And you wouldn't like to go back to St. Louis for just a little while, at least until you sort of get your bearings?"

"No, I just need to go."

"Don't forget me, Lucas. We've been through too much together."

"Dan, you aren't just part of my memories, you're

part of my very existence. I promise you, I won't forget you."

The two men shook hands, holding the grip a little longer than usual.

"I, uh, had better get going," Dan said. "I don't want to miss my train."

Lucas nodded, then turned away, he riding in one direction while Dan rode in the other.

SOME TIME LATER, Lucas found himself in the village of Taos, New Mexico. He heard music and laughter spilling out from one of the buildings, and a sign out front identified it as a cantina though there was no name for the establishment.

Lucas stopped his horse in front of a watering trough. "I don't care whether it has a name or not Charley, as long as they serve beer."

After Charley had drunk his fill, Lucas led him over to the cantina and tied him off to the hitching rail out front. It was cooler inside due to the lack of sun and to the half dozen evaporative coolers. As the large pots of water evaporated, the adjacent temperature was lowered by a few degrees.

The bartender was a heavy-set man with a black moustache, black hair, and brown eyes. "*Si, Señor?*" he said as Lucas stepped up to the bar.

"Do you have beer?"

"*Si.*"

"Then I'll have a beer."

Lucas watched as the bartender filled a mug with the golden liquid. He paid for it, took a long, satisfying drink, then turned his back to the bar to have a look around the place.

The clientele of the bar was a mixture of Anglos and Hispanics, though with considerably more Anglos. There were three men sitting at a table just in front of Lucas, having an intense conversation.

"They say the reward's worth five hunnert dollars now," one of the men said.

"Yeah? Well, I wouldn't go after the son of a bitch for a thousand dollars. Frank Baylor's a killer, he is. And to think, his mama's buried in our cemetery."

"What's that got to do with anything? Stella Baylor was as fine a woman as ever graced the streets of Taos and if she knowed what Frank done over in Valle Escondido she'd be turnin' over in her grave, I say."

"Well, somebody's got to stop him fore he kills another kid. The word is he kilt Asa Bloomfield, 'n a ten-year-old boy who just come in for a penny sack of candy," one of the men said. "Now that there's plum unholy."

"But do you think anybody's going after 'im. No. That's what I say."

"If you're so all fired upset, why don't you go down to the marshal's office and volunteer to ride after ole Frank?"

"'Cause I got me a wife and kids—that's why. Like you said, Frank Baylor is a killer."

"Excuse me," Lucas said, interrupting the conversation. "I'm sorry to be eavesdropping, but when did this happen? I think you said it involved a man named Frank Baylor. Was it here in Taos?"

"No, it was in Valle Escondido. It's no more 'n ten or twelve miles east of here. If you take the road east out of town, a few miles down the road you'll see a sign telling you which way to go."

Lucas nodded his head.

"Are you goin' after 'im?"

"That depends. What did you say the reward was?"

The men all laughed.

"What'd you say your name was?"

"I didn't say, but you didn't tell me the reward."

"Last we heard it's five hundred dollars, but after what he did in Valle Escondido, I'll bet them fine folks there added to the reward," one of the men said. "Folks don't take kindly to what he did."

"No, I wouldn't think they would. I believe I might just look up this Frank Baylor."

"I'll tell you this, Mister, if you find him, you'll have everyone's thanks."

Lucas smiled. "Thanks are nice, but I'd rather have the money."

The three men at the table laughed. "I reckon you would," one of them said.

Lucas nodded, set his mug down, then left the cantina. His first stop was the county courthouse. He intended to ask the sheriff to make him an unpaid deputy, but when he saw the office of a US Marshal, he had a better idea. If he could be appointed as a deputy US Marshal, his legal authority would be universal. He stepped into the marshal's office. "I'm Lucas Cain," he said as he extended his hand. "I'm sorry, Marshal, but I don't know your name."

"It's Urban. Dale Urban. What can I do for you?" the marshal asked.

"I'd like to be sworn in as a deputy US Marshal," Lucas replied.

Urban laughed. "That's very ambitious of you, Mr.

Cain. Even if I wanted a new deputy, I couldn't appoint you. I don't have the money for a deputy marshal."

"I don't want to be paid."

"What do you mean you don't want to be paid? Why would you want to be a deputy marshal if you aren't getting paid?"

"This is how I've worked in the past—in Missouri and Kansas and Colorado. If I'm not being paid, then I'm free to accept reward payment on any outlaws I catch."

The marshal laughed. "So what you're tellin' me is you want to be a bounty hunter."

"You could say that, but a lot of people don't like the idea of a bounty hunter. I've found if I have a badge, most people accept the idea of going after outlaws," Lucas said. "And to my way of thinking, if rewards weren't meant to be paid, they wouldn't be authorized."

"That's true," Urban said. "Do you have anyone in mind that you'd like to go after?"

"I just heard about Frank Baylor. He might be a good place to start."

Marshal Urban nodded. "He's a damn good one to start with. You're willing to serve without pay, you say?"

"Yes, sir."

"All right. I've never heard of such an arrangement, but I'm willing to give it a try, especially if it'll take a son of a bitch like Baylor out of circulation."

LUCAS RODE out of Taos with the authority of a deputy US Marshal. He was pretty sure he wouldn't actually find Baylor in Valle Escondido, but he had to start somewhere, and since this was where he had been told Baylor had committed the robbery and murder, it seemed the logical place to start.

THE TOWN of Valle Escondido was like most other southwestern towns. It had a central square that was flanked from either side by low, earth-colored adobe buildings.

There was no sheriff in Valle Escondido but there was a town marshal whose office Lucas found shared the post office building.

"Can I help you?" a man greeted. He was sitting at a table which had a stick lying on it. It was carved with the words city clerk.

"Yes, I would like to talk to the marshal, or one of his deputies," Lucas said.

The clerk chuckled. "There ain't no deputies. Our town marshal just stepped out back. Arnold Potter's his name."

When Potter came in, he was a rather large man, not muscular, but fat. The rolls in his chin made it appear as if he had no neck but merely a large head that sat directly on his shoulders. The marshal looked up when he saw Lucas.

"Somethin' I can do for you, Mister?" the marshal asked.

"You can give me a little information if you would," Lucas said.

"What do you wanna know?"

"I've been told that a man named Frank Baylor robbed a store and killed a young boy."

"That's right."

"How do you know it was Baylor who did it?"

"Because Asa Bloomfield, he's the one that owned the store that was robbed, lived long enough to tell us who done it."

"I'm glad to know there was a positive identification made, because I'm looking for Frank Baylor."

"You a law officer?"

Lucas wasn't wearing his star, so he pulled it from his pocket. "I'm a deputy US Marshal out of Taos."

"How come you ain't wearin' that star so's folks can see it?"

"I find it's easier to get folks to talk to me if I'm not wearing a badge."

"The way you come in here askin' about Baylor, I sort 'a figured you for a bounty hunter."

"Do you have something against bounty hunters?" Lucas asked.

"Yeah, I do," Potter said. "I've always considered a bounty hunter to be no better than a vigilante."

"I can see where someone might think that. But on the other hand, wouldn't you welcome someone who could bring in the man who killed a store clerk and a small boy?"

Marshal Potter grinned. "Well, I must say, it'd be good to see someone ridin' in with that son of a bitch, either sittin' in his saddle, or belly-down across it."

"I'll tell you how I normally work," Lucas said. "I'm a deputy US Marshal, but I'm serving without pay. That way I'm able to draw whatever bounty is being offered. And, this way the badge gives me some authority."

Potter smiled. "You're a smart one, ain't you? All right, go get that son of a bitch."

2

After Lucas left Marshal Potter's office, he got a bath and a haircut at the barbershop, then changed into his clean clothes. He walked back to the front carrying his dirty clothes.

"Do you have a laundry in this town, or do you know anyone who does washing?" he asked the barber.

"Yes, sir, my wife does that."

"Good. I need these done," Lucas said, holding up the clothes he was carrying.

"Leave 'em on the shelf back by the tub, and they'll be ready for you tomorrow," the barber said.

After leaving the barber shop, Lucas went into the mercantile next door. He immediately saw blood stains on the floor and a flush of anger came over him. He wondered if the blood was that of the boy Baylor had killed.

A young man barely into his teens stood behind the counter.

"What can I do for you, mister?"

"First off, tell me your name," Lucas said.

"It's Lawrence, but everybody calls me Larry. Larry Bloomfield."

Lucas started to tell the boy why he was in Valle Escondido but he decided not to.

"Well, Larry, I'm pleased to meet you," Lucas said as he extended his hand. "I need ammunition for my pistol and my rifle, and then I'll need some coffee, beans, and jerky."

"I can get those for you," Larry said as he began scurrying around the store. "Are you stayin' in these parts, mister?"

"Not for long, I hope. Is there a hotel in town?"

"Nope, but my ma's takin' in boarders, now that..." Larry stopped speaking. "Our place is down by the well."

Lucas gathered his purchases and put them in his saddlebags. Leading Charley toward the well, he saw a house that said, "Rooms." When he went inside, there was a moment he felt as if he had just made an unauthorized entry into someone's home. The room looked like the parlor of any house with a sofa, chairs, and a table. There was no check-in desk, nor was there anything else that would suggest this to be a business. He was about to leave when a heavy-set woman with white hair tied back in a bun came into the room.

"Do you need a place to sleep?" she asked.

"Yes, ma'am. Larry said you were letting rooms."

"I am. It'll be twenty-five cents a night," the woman answered, "and that don't include no eats."

Lucas smiled, as he handed her a quarter. "And where would you tell me I can find a bite?"

"Across the plaza."

THE NEXT MORNING, he crossed the plaza to have his breakfast. There was a small sign on the door saying Jack's Restaurant. Marshal Potter was there, and seeing Lucas come in, he invited him to join him at his table.

"Thanks," Lucas said as he sat down.

"You'll be starting after Baylor today?"

"Yeah, I wanted to sleep in a real bed and have one last meal before I start living on beans, bacon, and jerky for a while."

"Well, I can't say as I blame you. Did you stay with Mattie?" Potter asked. He poured coffee into the empty cup that sitting in front of Lucas.

"I didn't get her name, but Larry told me it was his ma's place."

"That's her. Poor woman. I don't know what she and that boy are going to do without Asa," Potter said. "I hope they don't have to pull up stakes and go someplace else, but it's gonna be hard to make a livin' without her man."

"What's good here?" Lucas asked, changing the subject.

Potter chuckled, and patted his belly. "Well, as you can tell, everything's good here. My problem is, I tend to eat too much of it at the same time."

Lucas laughed.

When a young woman came to the table, Lucas ordered steak, eggs, potatoes, and biscuits.

"Darlin', we'll need another pot of coffee, too," Potter said, holding out the nearly empty coffee pot.

"So, tell me, Cain, when did you start this bounty hunting? I know you don't want to call it that, but that's what it is."

"I started when I was a policeman."

"A policeman? You mean you were somewhere where a law officer could collect bounties?"

"Not really. If you were a policeman in my home town, fees for specific actions like when you would serve a delinquent summons or when you made an arrest were the only way you got paid. So I made an arrangement not to get paid for anything. It worked out well for me."

"And you had the authority of the law. I can see now what you meant by being an unpaid deputy US Marshal."

After they finished breakfast, the two men had just stepped out of the restaurant when a man on horseback came riding into town at full speed.

Because of the way the rider had galloped into town, several of the town's citizens had come out to see what was going on. When the rider saw Marshal Potter in front of the restaurant, he jerked his horse to a stop and called out to him.

"Marshal! Marshal Potter!"

Others, seeing the rider stop and dismount, joined the gathering crowd, to satisfy their own curiosity, resulting in a group of about ten people standing around the marshal.

"Ennis, look at this poor animal. You nearly killed 'im," Potter scolded as he began patting the horse's neck. "What on earth's gotten in to you?"

"It's Mr. McCord," Ennis said.

"Jason McCord? What about him? What's happened?"

"He's gone," Ennis said.

"Gone? What do you mean gone? Good heavens! You don't mean he's died do you?"

"No. Leastwise, I don't think so. At least not yet," Ennis said. "But this mornin' 'afore it was daylight even, three men come out to the ranch and well, they...they..."

"They what, man? Speak up!"

"They took him."

"Took him?"

"Yes, sir, at gunpoint it was. They just kicked open the door of the house, went inside and took him."

"And nobody did anything?"

"We couldn't do nothin'," Ennis explained. "We was all asleep in the bunkhouse and didn't know nothin' about it, 'till it was too late. When we heard Mrs. McCord a yellin', we all run out front to see what was goin' on. When we did, we found ourselves lookin' down the barrels of a couple of guns. The two of 'em that wasn't takin' Mr. McCord, was in the front of the bunkhouse just waitin' on us. There we was, standin' out front in our underwear without no guns or nothin', and there them two was, sittin' on their horses, holdin' their guns pointed at us, just as big as all get out."

"Did you recognize any of them?" Potter asked.

"Only one of 'em. Him that took Mr. McCord out of the house, with a gun held up against Mr. McCord's head. We all of us recognized him."

"Well, who was it, man? Quit stallin' and spit it out," Potter demanded.

Ennis paused for a moment as if for dramatic effect, before he answered.

"It was Frank Baylor."

"Baylor?" Potter said.

The name was repeated by several in the crowd, to make sure that everyone heard it.

"Look here, Ennis, are you sure it was Frank Baylor?" Potter asked.

"Yeah, I'm damn sure," Ennis replied. "If you remember, he used to work for Mr. McCord, 'n he slept in the same bunkhouse with the rest of us."

A man stepped forward from the crowd.

"You plannin' on sendin' anyone after Baylor?"

"This is Drew Hunsinger," Potter said, identifying the man who had stepped forward. "He used to be the Taos County sheriff, 'till he got hisself married 'n bought 'im a small farm."

"I'm going after him," Lucas said.

"Drew, this is Lucas Cain," Marshal Potter said. "He's one of Dale Urban's marshals."

"All right, Cain, if you're goin' after him, I'll go with you," Hunsinger said.

Hunsinger was a man in his late thirties to early forties. There was a solid look about him, the look of someone who would be dependable and trustworthy, but Lucas didn't see the hard-edge a man would need to go up against someone like Frank Baylor.

Lucas studied Hunsinger for a long moment trying to decide whether taking him along would be a help or a hindrance. He was certain that the former sheriff's intentions were good, and he believed he could trust him. But years of living on the edge had given him the unique ability to judge others, not only their character, but their potential. Drew Hunsinger passed the character test but failed the potential. Lucas knew that if he took him with him, at some critical point Hunsinger would think of his wife, and that distraction could get him killed.

"No," he said. "I appreciate the offer, but I work better alone."

"Are you crazy? Ennis said there was Baylor and two more. How is one man going to go up against three men?"

"Two men wouldn't make the odds much better," Lucas replied. "One man is more likely to slip through.

Also, if I'm by myself, there's no need for me to be worrying about the other man. Believe me, Hunsinger, I know what I'm doing. I've been in situations like this before."

"Yeah, I'm sure you have," Hunsinger replied a bit caustically.

"He's right, Drew," Potter said. "If you'd just stop for a moment and think about it, you know damn well Edna wouldn't want you doing this."

Hunsinger sighed, then took off his hat and ran his hand through his hair.

"I know I'm not the sheriff anymore, but I just can't lay down the responsibility. And I especially can't just stand by and see friends get in trouble and not try to help," Hunsinger said. "And Jason McCord is a good man."

"You have another responsibility now," Potter said.

"Yeah, you're right. I don't like admittin' it, but you're right," Hunsinger said.

"Ennis," Lucas said, turning to the man who was still astride his horse, "would you take me out to the ranch to meet Mrs. McCord?"

"Why do you want to meet her? She's real upset right now."

"If I'm going after Baylor, I need to get as much information as I can."

"All right, come on, but you better not be makin' her more upset than she already is."

FRANK BAYLOR, Sid Mobley, and Aaron Todd were encamped in a thicket of trees about three miles from the McCord house. McCord, bound head and foot, was with them.

"You think McCord's old lady will come up with the fifteen hundred dollars?" Mobley asked.

"She will, if she wants her husband back in one piece," Baylor said.

"We don't have that much cash on hand," McCord said.

"I know your wife from when I used to work for you. I know she's the one who takes care of all your business. If she don't have the money, I know she'll find a way to get it."

"Hey, Baylor, what if she don't want him back?" Todd asked with a little chuckle. "Hell, if we kill 'im, we might be doin' her a favor."

"No, I remember her. She'll do whatever it takes to get 'im back," Baylor said.

"Maybe we should'a asked for more," Mobley suggested.

"I don't think she can raise no more 'n fifteen hunnert dollars," Baylor said. "That's five hunnert dollars apiece, 'n that's a hell of lot better than the hunnert 'n twenty dollars I got from robbin' that store."

"And for that, you killed Asa Bloomfield and young Timmy Malone," McCord said.

"Yeah, I did. But that's goin' to work out well for me," Baylor said with an evil smile.

"And just how do you figure that?" McCord asked.

"Easy. Your wife will know that if I didn't mind killin' a kid, I sure as hell won't mind killin' you, if she don't come up with the money."

ABOUT FIVE MILES away from where Baylor and the others were encamped, Lucas and Ennis were on their way out to the McCord Ranch. Because Ennis had run his horse all the way into town, the trip back to the ranch took almost half an hour. When they arrived, they dismounted in front of the ranch house. Lucas followed Ennis up onto the porch, where Ennis knocked on the door.

The woman who opened the door looked to be in her mid to late forties. Her features were somewhat distorted as the result of a lot of crying.

"Mrs. McCord, this is Marshal Lucas Cain. He wants to talk to you."

"Oh, Ennis, you talk to him, I can't talk to anyone right now."

"Mrs. McCord, I intend to find your husband and get him back to you," Lucas said, "but, in order to do that, I'll need any information you can give me."

Mrs. McCord stepped back from the door. "Then come in. Sit anywhere." There was a soiled handkerchief on the table by the chair where Mrs. McCord sat, and she picked it up, then blew her nose. "What do you need to know?"

"Your hand said he believed it was Frank Baylor who took your husband."

"It was Baylor, all right."

"How can you be so sure?"

"Because Frank Baylor used to work for us. I remember him."

"Ennis also said there were two men with Baylor. Do you have any idea who those two men were?"

Mrs. McCord shook her head. "No, I didn't get a good look at them. I guess they were out by the bunkhouse."

"Why do you think Baylor took your husband? You said he used to work for you. Do you think it might have been to settle some old score?"

"It could be. Jason fired him."

"Oh? Why was he fired, may I ask?"

"We had no way of proving it but we're sure that he was stealing cows from us. Then, when he robbed Mr. Bloomfield's store and killed him and that sweet little boy, it just reinforced our belief that he had stolen our cows."

"Do you think the firing is why he took your husband?"

"I suppose this is important." She picked up a folded piece of paper from the table where the handkerchief had been, then handed it to Lucas.

Lucas read the note. "He and the other two are holding your husband for a fifteen-hundred-dollar ransom. Forgive me for asking, but do you have that much money?"

"No," Mrs. McCord said. Tears began to flow again, and once more she began dabbing at her eyes. "That's why I'm so worried. I fear that if I don't give him the money, he'll kill Jason."

"If you did have the money, how are you supposed to deliver it?"

"I'm supposed to leave the money at our line shack. When he gets the money, he said he'll turn Jason loose."

"Did he insist that you deliver the money yourself? Or can someone do it for you?"

"He didn't say. He just said that I have one day to get the money to him or he'll kill Jason. But I don't have the money, and I'm so afraid." Again, she dabbed at her eyes.

"I have the money," Lucas said. "I'll get your husband back for you."

"I...I don't understand. Why would you use your own money to get my husband back?"

"Let's just say that I'm baiting the hook," Lucas replied.

3

When Lucas returned to town, he went to the marshal's office.

"Did you see Mrs. McCord?" Potter asked.

"I saw her."

"How's she doing?"

"As I'm sure you can imagine, she's taking it pretty hard, but I get the idea that she's a strong woman. I think she can hold on until I get her husband back to her."

"So you're going to try and get him back are you?"

"I'm not just going to try, I'm going to do it," Lucas said.

"Well, I sure hope you can. Jason McCord is good man."

"Do you have a map of the county?" Lucas asked.

"Yes, over here on the wall."

"Can you point out McCord's line shack?"

"Yeah, I can do that. It's right here," Potter said, pointing to a spot on the map."

"Have you ever been there?"

"Yeah, I've been there a few times."

"Tell me about what's around the line shack."

"What do you mean, what's around it?"

"Trees, hills, rocks."

"Well the cabin sits right here, on the Gallinas River," Potter said as he pointed to the map. "This area here is flat grazing land. But there are trees here, and Wheeler Peak here, has a ridge of rocks and boulders that come right down to the river."

Lucas smiled. "Thank you, Marshal Potter. I can work with that."

TWO HOURS LATER, Lucas arrived at the line shack sitting as Potter had described, on the banks of the Gallinas River. He didn't see any horses so he figured they must be somewhere observing the shack, waiting for the ransom. Then he saw someone come out of the cabin to relieve himself, then go back inside. He didn't know if everyone was in the cabin or if it was just that one man. However, since there were no horses in sight, he decided the man must be alone. McCord could be in there as well, but he doubted that.

Lucas rode down to the cabin, then dismounted and took the satchel down.

Aaron Todd was inside looking through the window. He walked over and jerked the door open.

"You got the money with you?"

"Oh!" Lucas said in a voice that he hoped sounded frightened. "I didn't think anyone would be in here."

"What did you think? That we was just gonna have somebody drop off the money and leave it, unguarded? You do have the money, don't you?"

"Y-yes, I—uh, I've got it here," Lucas said, trying to show fear to the man.

"All right, bring it in here," Todd said, stepping back from the door.

"Y-you want me to come inside? I thought all I had to do was leave the money and you'd let Mr. McCord go."

Todd drew his pistol and pointed it at Lucas. "I said, bring the money inside."

"All right. The money's here, every dollar you asked for." Lucas stepped inside, then looked around.

"W-where's Mr. McCord?"

"Ha! You really think we're goin' to let him go? We've kept 'im alive just long enough to get the money. But he ain't leavin' here alive, 'n neither are you."

Todd pointed his pistol at Lucas and started to thumb back the hammer. The evil smile on his face turned to shock when Lucas tossed the satchel toward him, and as Todd moved to avoid the satchel, Lucas drew his own gun and fired, doing so before Todd could even pull the trigger. Todd dropped his pistol and slapped his hand over the hole in his chest. That was the last voluntary movement of his life, because he had been shot in the heart. He fell to the floor.

Lucas made sure the man was dead, then he put his pistol back in his holster and opened the door. As he staggered back outside, he held his hand over his stomach, took a few steps forward, then fell face down.

"HA! DID YOU SEE THAT?" Mobley asked. "Todd kilt the son of a bitch."

"Yeah, well I hope it's not because he didn't have the money with him," Baylor replied.

"Why, you know he did. We seen 'im carryin' the satchel in."

"Let's go down there and see," Baylor said. He turned his attention to McCord, who was still bound hand and foot, sitting against a tree. "You better pray that this man Todd killed brought the money. Because, if he didn't, there's no reason to keep you alive."

"You never were worth a damn, Baylor," McCord said. "I should have fired you a long time ago."

"You say I'm not worth a damn, but you better hope you're worth fifteen hunnert dollars. Come on, Sid, let's go see if he brought the money."

WHEN LUCAS INITIALLY FELL, he did so, hoping that if Baylor had been watching this might draw him out. He was on the ground only for a moment when he heard voices. They were too far away and too indistinct for him to be able to understand what they were saying, but he was pretty sure that it would be Baylor, and the third man.

As the two men came closer, Lucas could hear their conversation.

"If the money ain't there, are we goin' to kill McCord anyway?"

"Yeah."

"But if we kill 'im, then we won't have nothin' to hold over 'em to get the money."

"Use your head, Mobley. If they didn't bring the money this time, they're not goin' to."

"Yeah, I guess you're right. Hey, what do you say we just go off 'n leave the son of a bitch tied to a tree,"

Mobley said with a laugh. "If a wolf or a bear don't kill 'im, then he'll just starve to death."

"No, I intend to see that he's dead before we leave. I don't want to take no chances that he might get out of here alive."

LUCAS REMAINED VERY STILL, until he knew that the two men were right over him.

"Todd! Todd, come on out here, and bring the money with you."

There was a moment of silence.

"Hey, Baylor, you don't reckon Todd run off with the money, do you?"

"How would he run? His horse is up there with ours. Let's have a look at this son of a bitch," Baylor said.

Baylor reached down to roll Lucas over on his back.

"You reckon he's dead?" Todd asked.

"We'll just make sure," Baylor replied.

It was awkward for Lucas to draw his gun while lying down, but there was no need for speed as Baylor and Mobley made no attempt to draw their guns quickly.

"Surprise," Lucas said, lifting his gun and shooting both Baylor and Mobley before they could draw their own guns.

Lucas got to his feet, made certain that both Baylor and Mobley were dead, then he started into the trees.

"Jason! Jason McCord, your wife sent me to get you," Lucas yelled. "Baylor and his men are dead. Give me a shout if you can hear me."

"I'm here!" McCord shouted.

Lucas followed the sound of the voice until he saw McCord sitting on the ground, leaning up against a tree.

His feet were tied, and his hands were tied behind him. Pulling his knife, Lucas began cutting him free.

IT WAS A VERY happy reunion between McCord and his wife. Mrs. McCord insisted that Lucas stay for supper, so he did.

Ennis and the others who rode for the brand, were out front studying the bodies of Baylor, Mobley, and Todd, who were tied to their horses lying belly down.

"Damn," one of the ranch hands said. "Cain kilt all three of 'em. How'd he do that?"

"I don't know how he done it, but he sure did," Ennis said. "I want to stay on his good side."

WHEN LUCAS TOOK the three bodies into town, Marshall Potter was as surprised as McCord's men had been. But as it turned out, Lucas was also surprised—pleasantly so. In addition to the five-hundred-dollar reward for Baylor, Mobley and Todd were worth two hundred fifty dollars each. Lucas left town a thousand dollars richer than when he arrived. He decided he would go back to Valle Escondido to call on Mattie Bloomfield. Mattie and Larry deserved some of this money. If it made things a little better for them, Lucas would be pleased.

4

After leaving Valle Escondido, Lucas spent time wandering through the New Mexico countryside enjoying the table-topped mesas and the red and yellow cliffs. He enjoyed looking up at the boundless sky with stars so crisp it seemed as if he could touch them. He explored pueblos where Indians had lived for hundreds of years, and yet now he knew the Indians were scattered to various reservations set up by the government.

Lucas felt a kinship with the Indians. He knew he was a man with battle scars. Although some of them were visible—a saber scar from the battle of Shiloh, lash scars across his back from his time as a prisoner of war in Andersonville—his most severe scars weren't visible. These were the scars on his soul, from watching his friends slain on the battlefields of the Civil War, to losing his wife and baby during child birth, and more recently to the things he had seen while pursuing outlaws.

With his supplies running low, he saw a settlement not far to the south. When he reached the little town he saw a sign saying, Sweetwater, New Mexico. The smells emanating from one of the buildings caused his appetite to be stimulated. It had been nearly a week since he had eaten anything he hadn't prepared over a campfire, and the thought of sitting down to an actual meal was very welcome.

But before he would let himself eat, he wanted to step in to meet the sheriff and make himself known. He had never been in Sweetwater, so he didn't know anything about the town or the sheriff. From his first impression, the town looked like a sleepy little village without a lot of mischief, but he had learned things were not always as they seemed.

It was easy to locate the sheriff's office, because it had a sign hung above the door. He dismounted and patted his horse on his neck.

"Well, Charley, what kind of welcome will we get here?" he asked, as he tied Charley off at the hitching rail. Because Lucas was on his own so much of the time, he and Charley had developed a relationship that was far more than that of horse and rider. There was a symbiotic synergy between them that was as close as two friends.

There was a man sitting behind his desk cleaning a rifle and he looked up when Lucas approached his desk.

"Howdy, Mister."

"Are you the sheriff?" Lucas asked.

"Yes, sir, Sheriff Leonard Greenly. What can I do for you?"

"Sheriff, my name is Lucas Cain."

"Lucas Cain? It seems like I've heard that name," the sheriff said. "Would you be that Marshal who went after that no-account Frank Baylor over in Valle Escondido?"

"I did bring in Frank Baylor," Lucas said.

The sheriff stood, and extended his hand. "Am I glad to see you."

"You are?" Though he had been a little surprised by the sheriff's recognition of him, the sheriff's positive reaction surprised him even more.

"You're here after Ed Meachum, ain't ya?"

"Well, I could be. Who's Ed Meachum?"

"That's strange. I thought you was comin' here to tell me you was going after 'im. There's a five-hundred-dollar reward for him, dead or alive. And if you want me to be honest with you, well, I reckon most folks here about would just as soon see you bring him in draped over the back of his horse."

"What did Meachum do?"

"The son of a bitch killed Chris Anderson and his wife and their little four-year-old girl."

"Can you be sure it was Meachum who killed them?"

"Well, nobody saw 'im do it, but Chris' brother Toby was in the henhouse when Meachum rode up. There's bad blood between them two, and Toby decided to lay low. He heard the gunshots, though."

"That sounds like a pretty good witness to me. Did he get to speak to his brother before he died? To maybe get an idea why Meachum would kill a man in cold blood."

"And his wife and little girl," the sheriff added shaking his head. "That was a mighty solemn funeral when we buried 'em. Put all three of 'em in the same grave. We thought Chris would have wanted that."

"But you don't know why Meachum would kill these people?"

"No, no reason," Greenley said. "Now if it had been Toby, maybe we could have seen it, but there warn't a nicer man in this county than Chris Anderson. And Wanda, well she baked the best cakes for the church socials. Why Meachum would want to kill them is beyond anything anybody can think of."

"Do you know anything that would help me find Meachum? A description, maybe?"

"He's not very big, maybe five foot five or so, 'n I don't reckon he weighs much over a hundred-thirty pounds. But the easiest way to recognize him is he got the earlobe of his left ear bit off the last time he was in a fight."

"That's something that's a little different," Lucas said.

"You goin' after 'im?"

"Absolutely."

"When will you head out?"

"I'll get started first thing in the morning. Tonight, I'd like a couple of beers, a meal I don't cook, and a bed to sleep on."

"Huck's Saloon for your beer, Suzie's Kitchen for your supper and also for your bed. She'll put your horse up, too, for an extra dime."

Lucas smiled. "Sounds good. I'll give them a try."

THE FIRST PLACE Lucas visited after leaving Sheriff Greenley's office was Suzie's Kitchen and Rooming House.

"Are you a eatin' or a sleepin'?" a very pleasant middle-aged woman asked.

"How about both," Lucas replied as he signed the guest book. "And I was told you have a place for my horse, too."

"I do. You can take him around back and put him in the corral. Benny will take care of him—rub him down and give him a sack of feed, then put him in the shed."

"And how much will that be?" Lucas asked.

"Two bits," the woman said.

Lucas smiled again recalling that the sheriff had said taking care of the horse would be a dime. "Two bits, it is."

After leaving his bedroll in a tiny room with one of the smallest beds he had ever seen, he went back to get a bite to eat. As it was early in the afternoon, Lucas was the only one in the little room that served as the restaurant.

"I didn't get your name," Lucas said as the woman came to get his order.

"Don't Suzie's Kitchen tell you nothing?"

Lucas laughed out loud, realizing he hadn't had a real laugh in a long time.

"I guess you put one over on me, Suzie."

"I'll say, but my whole name's Suzie Greenley."

Still smiling, Lucas nodded. "The sheriff?"

"Yes, sir, he's my man. Now what can I get for you?"

"I should ask what do you have?"

"I think I got some taters and roast beef and gravy left over from dinner. If you don't want that, I can get up some ham and eggs."

"The roast beef sounds perfect."

WHEN LUCAS LEFT SUZIE'S, he walked down to the other end of the block to Huck's Saloon. The interior of the saloon surprised him. There was a soft, golden light coming from a gleaming chandelier and the atmosphere seemed quite congenial. There were a couple men standing at one end of the bar, engaged in a friendly conversation, while at the other end, the bartender stayed busy pouring drinks and cleaning glasses. The four tables were filled with cowboys and what appeared to be shopkeepers. They were all laughing and exchanging stories, while one attractive young woman seemed to flirt with each of them as she made her way from table to table refreshing drinks as they were called for.

Because it was mid-June, the two heating stoves were now cold, though there continued to hang in the air the distinctive aroma of wood smoke from their winter's activity. Mixed with that scent were the smells of liquor, tobacco, and the occasional odor of men, too long at work with too few baths.

"What'll it be?" the bartender asked.

"A beer would be nice."

"Comin' to stay, or passin' through."

"Well, I wouldn't say either one," Lucas answered as he picked up the beer.

"That's a strange answer," the bartender said, and then he saw the badge that was pinned to Lucas's shirt. "Are you after somebody?"

"Yes, I am," Lucas said, taking another drink.

"Well, I hope you're 'a lookin' for that son of a bitch that kilt Chris Anderson 'n his wife and little girl."

"That would be Ed Meachum?"

"Yeah, that's him all right."

"Sheriff Greenley just told me about Meachum, and he will be my target while I'm here."

"Where do you come from?"

Lucas took a deep breath. "Missouri, originally, but I travel around a lot."

"Probably most of the folks who live in New Mexico are from someplace else."

"I don't suppose you have any idea where I might go to look for Ed Meachum, do you?" Lucas asked.

"He used to work for a fella over in Turqui. That's the only place I've ever heard of him being somewhere," the bartender said.

"Thanks," Lucas said, finishing his beer.

SOME DISTANCE AWAY FROM SWEETWATER, in Mascoran, Ed Meachum dismounted in front of the High Dollar Saloon. Just before he went into the saloon, he saw a board on the building with reward posters pinned on it.

WANTED
FOR MURDER
DEAD OR ALIVE
ED MEACHUM
$500 REWARD

Meachum pulled the dodger down, wadded it up, and stuck it in his pocket. Then he went into the saloon. He had never been here before, so he thought it was most likely he wouldn't see anyone who knew him.

Everything seemed to go well at first. He was standing at the bar, nursing his second whiskey and wondering where he was going to get some more money. He knew that the twenty-seven dollars he had taken from Chris Anderson wouldn't go very far.

"Hello, George," the bartender said to a man who had just stepped up to the bar. "Mollie let you off early, did she?"

"That she did," George said with a laugh. "I think the Emporium belongs to me, but it's really hers. She decides when it's open and when it's closed, so she closed the door and sent me on my way."

"I thought she always made you sweep up after the day was over."

"Oh, she did that, but now she's over there counting money and she doesn't like me around when she's doing that."

The bartender chuckled. "I don't blame her. I always did think she's the smart one."

"She probably is, but I told her if it wasn't for me, she wouldn't have any money to count in the first place."

Meachum smiled as he finished his whiskey. Then he left the saloon and saw a sign saying Blum's Emporium right across the street. He headed for the store.

There was a closed sign posted on the front door, so Meachum went between Blum's and the next-door building, until he reached the alley. Then coming up behind Blum's he was prepared to force his way into the store, when he got a lucky break. The back door wasn't locked.

Moving through to the front of the store, he saw a woman sitting at a table behind the counter. She had a little stack of money beside her and she was making entries in a book. So intent was she on her task, that she didn't see Meachum until he was right upon her.

"What are you doing here?" she asked, in a startled voice. "The store's closed."

Without a word, Meachum stepped up to her, grabbed her from behind, put his left hand over her mouth, then slashed her throat. As she lay on the floor bleeding and flopping around, he took the money from the table. The amount she had recorded in the book was one hundred-forty-three dollars.

5

The first thing Lucas did when he rode into Mascoran was stop at the saloon for a beer. As long as he was here, he figured he may as well inquire of the bartender, about Ed Meachum.

"Yeah, I've heard of him," the bartender in the High Dollar Saloon said, answering Lucas's question. "He used to work for Vernon Jacoby, 'n he was worthless, even then. When he left town, ever'one said good riddance, but Andy Carter said that he seen him last week so now we know the son of a bitch come back to town. Then, not long after Andy seen Meachum, someone killed Mollie Blum 'n stole all the money from the store, and there ain't nobody in town but what don't think that it was Meachum who done it."

"Mollie Blum?"

"Yeah, she was George Blum's wife, 'n they used to run Blum's Emporium. I say they used to, but truth is, George is still runnin' it."

"I'm looking for Meachum. Do you think Mr. Blum would talk to me?" Lucas asked.

"If he knows you're after Meachum, he will, you damn right," the bartender answered.

A LITTLE BELL on the door announced Lucas's arrival when he went into Blum's Emporium. Although it was mid-afternoon, the store appeared to be empty. There was a man sitting behind the counter, and Lucas didn't think he had ever seen a more sorrowful expression than the one showing in the man's face. Because of that, Lucas surmised that this must be George Blum.

"Mr. Blum, I wonder if you would talk to me about what happened to your wife."

"You aren't some newspaper man, are you?" Blum said. "Because I don't want Mollie's story talked about. She wouldn't like that."

"No, sir, I'm a deputy US Marshal. I don't wish to cause you any discomfort over talking about what happened, but I'm looking for Ed Meachum. He was placed at the scene of a murder in Sweetwater, and I was told he once worked on a ranch near here. If you could tell me anything you might know about him, I'd appreciate it," Lucas said.

"I don't know any more about him than you know, and nobody actually saw him..."

"I understand," Lucas said. "Did anyone see him leave town?"

"The only one who recognized him was Andy Carter, a fellow who used to work with him out at Jacoby's place. He said he saw him headin' south when he hightailed it out of here," George said. "He figured he was headin' for Sapello."

"Thanks, that's somewhere to start. And, Mr. Blum,

I'm sorry about your wife. I lost my own wife, so I know how hard it is."

"Did your wife get her throat cut?" George looked at Lucas with a hard look on his face. "Did you walk in and find her when she didn't come home?"

"No."

"Then you can't really relate to what I'm goin' through, now, can you?"

"No, sir, if you put it like that, I suppose you're right. But I am sorry."

George took a deep breath. "No, it's me who should say I'm sorry. I shouldn't have jumped on you like I did. It's just Mollie was..." He stopped and then continued. "Just find the son of a bitch and see that he pays for what he did to my Mollie and to the one he killed in Sweetwater."

"It was three—a man, his wife, and their four-year old daughter," Lucas said. "I promise you I'll find Ed Meachum."

LUCAS'S next stop was Sapello, and there he learned that he was only a day behind Meachum. When he described him as a small man with a missing left earlobe, he was easy to identify.

"We don't have telegraph service here," the town marshal said, "so I had no idea he was a wanted man. But as far as I know, he left town yesterday. If I was you, I'd look for 'im down south a bit. Probably headin' for Mexico."

"Thanks, you've been a big help."

A HOT BREATH of air blew across the valley, leaving a cloud of dust hanging in the air to glow red in the sun. One could almost think that they were looking at the very fires of Hades, and could expect Old Scratch himself to make a sudden appearance.

But it wasn't Old Scratch who fired the shot from behind a rock. Lucas Cain heard Charley give a quick whinny of pain, then collapse. He managed to leap from the saddle in time to avoid being trapped beneath him.

"Ha! You ain't a' goin' to be chasin' me no more now, are ya?" Ed Meachum shouted from behind the rock.

Lucas didn't answer.

"What's the matter? Ain't you got nothin' to say?" Meachum asked, shouting as before.

Lucas waited, each labored breath of his dying horse tearing at his very soul.

"Damn, you're trapped under your horse, ain't ya?" Meachum said, laughing at the idea.

"Well, don't worry, I'll finish you off. I'll go ahead 'n put you 'n your horse both out of your misery, 'cause I'm just that kind of a feller."

Lucas lay quietly, listening as Meachum approached. Then, just before Meachum reached him, Lucas set up.

"You killed my horse, you son of a bitch," Lucas said quietly, just before he pulled the trigger.

Meachum went down, with a bullet in his heart.

Lucas put his hand on his horse's face, just as he drew his last breath.

"Charley, my old friend. What am I going to do without you?"

Lucas swallowed the lump in his throat and blinked his eyes a couple of times to stop the tears.

Lucas Cain shook his canteen to gauge the amount of water remaining and determined that it was almost empty. He had already transferred the water from Ed Meachum's canteen to his own, but that still left him with very little water.

Meachum's horse was still alive, but it was displaying the signs of severe mistreatment. The horse's ribs were showing and he had a vacant look in his eyes. Lucas knew that the horse wouldn't be strong enough to carry him and Meachum's body, so he didn't even try.

When he had left Sapello, Lucas had not veered from the main road. He decided his best bet was to wait for the next traffic to come along.

He waited about an hour and a half, then even as he drained the last of his water, he saw a column of dust indicating an approaching stagecoach.

Lucas stood where he was for about ten more minutes, then as the coach approached, he stepped out into the road and held up both hands to show that he wasn't holding a gun.

He could hear the hoof beats of the horses and the squeak and rattle of the coach as it drew closer. Then he heard the driver give the command for the six-horse team to stop.

"Mister, you look like you need a ride," the driver said.

"Yes, sir, I truly do."

"How come? I see a horse standin' over there."

"I don't think he's strong enough to carry me and the body."

"Body? What body?"

"The one lying over there," Lucas said, pointing. "I need to get him into town."

"Mister, you ain't goin' to be throwin' no dead body

on this here stagecoach. I got passengers, includin' a woman and a little boy," the driver said.

"I won't have to put him on the coach. I can drape him across his horse and tie him on to back of the coach."

"Well, all right, if you do it like that, I don't reckon he'll be any trouble. But it's goin' to cost you a dollar 'n a half to tie that horse on. Why's it so important you get him into town, anyway? If you want to just bury 'im out here, I'll wait."

Lucas shook his head. "No, sir, he's going into town to the sheriff's office. This is Ed Meachum and I aim to collect the reward on him."

"Ed Meachum?" the driver said. "That's the body you got?"

"That's the one," Lucas said.

"Mister, you go ahead 'n tie the horse onto the back of the coach. I'll haul that son of a bitch in for free."

"Thanks," Lucas said.

Lucas walked over to where Meachum lay, and picking him up easily, he draped him over the saddle. Using the dead man's own rope, he tied Meachum's feet to his hands underneath the horse, securing the load.

Then, taking the reins, he led the horse over to the back of the coach. As he was tying the horse on to the coach, a dandified-looking man climbed out of the coach, then walked around to join Lucas.

"Did I hear you say this was Ed Meachum? The one who shot that family in Sweetwater?"

"He's the one," Lucas said, "and he also killed a woman in Mascoran."

"Oh, my," the man said. "I hadn't heard about the woman." He followed Lucas back up to the door of the coach.

"Driver?" he called up to the man who was waiting patiently on the driver's box. "I'll be paying this gentleman's fare."

"That's all right by me," the driver replied as Lucas and the man climbed into the coach.

The passengers in the coach included two other men, in addition to the man who had offered to pay Lucas's fare, an attractive young woman who appeared to be in her late twenties, and a boy of about eight or nine. Lucas nodded respectfully at the woman, and her return of the nod was barely perceptible. One of the men was considerably overweight, and he sat holding a case on his lap. Lucas figured he was probably a drummer. The remaining passenger was a gambler whom Lucas had run into in Colorado. They exchanged a silent greeting.

The dandified man identified himself. "I'm Gerald Colson and I'm the editor for the *Santa Fe New Mexican*. Would you tell me what happened, if you don't mind?"

"Meachum shot my horse and I shot him."

Colson was surprised and perplexed by the short answer.

"That's all there is to it?" Colson asked.

"That's it," Lucas said.

"There has to be more than that. Had you been on his trail for a long time? And was there a shoot-out between the two of you? Did you know the people he killed? Look, mister, I want a story, here."

"I told you what happened. He shot my horse, I shot him."

"My, but you are a man of few words," Colson said.

"Yes," the gambler said with a wide grin. "But if you knew who you were talking to, you'd know he is indeed a man of few words."

"That's just it. I don't know this gentleman's name," Colson said.

"Oh, well, let me introduce you then," the gambler said. "Mr. Colson, this is Lucas Cain."

"How are you doing, Ristine?" Lucas said.

"Cain," Ristine replied with a nod and a broad smile.

"Wow! Are you the one who saved all those ranches up in Colorado? William Lightfoot is a friend of mine, and I read the glowing article he wrote about you in the *Higbee Ledger*," Colson said.

"If you read the article, you know I didn't save the ranches. I just told them how to have the railroad pay to use their land," Lucas said.

"What a modest man," Colson continued. "That's not how Lightfoot described it."

"It doesn't matter. There will be no story about Ed Meachum. At least not one that comes from me."

Normally, the stage coach would arrive in town with the horses at a gallop to "make an entry." Such an arrival would call attention to the stage coach, and that attention would be good for the company as well.

This arrival, though at a leisurely pace, drew more attention than any coach that came into town at a gallop, because everyone saw a horse tied to the back of the coach and more specifically, the body that was draped across it.

"WHAT DO YOU MEAN, you're putting in for the reward?" the town marshal asked. "You're a lawman, you ain't able to collect no reward."

"Yes, I can," Lucas said. He showed the marshal his letter of appointment from US Marshal Dale Urban. In the letter it explained that as Lucas Cain was an unpaid deputy, he was authorized to collect the bounties on any wanted person he brought in.

"FOUR HUNDRED SIXTY, four hundred eighty, five hundred dollars," Marshal Dixon said, counting out the reward money he had just picked up from the bank. He slid the money across the desk to Lucas.

"Well, that closes the books on Edward Meachum, and we're all better off because of it," Dixon said. "I've already wired Sheriff Greenley. He'll let everybody know that you took care of Meachum."

"And let the sheriff in Mascoran know, too," Lucas said, as he picked up the money.

"So tell me, Cain, what are you going to do next? Are you going back up north?"

"I'm not sure where I'll be heading," Lucas said. "I'd like to look through your wanted posters, if you don't mind."

"I don't mind at all."

"Thanks," Lucas said as he perused the dodgers the sheriff had posted on his bulletin board.

"Here's one with a thousand dollar reward," Lucas said after a moment or two.

"Yeah, you must be talking about Dudley Stewart," Dixon said. "He's a bad one all right. We've been tryin' to run him down better part of a year."

"Thanks for the tip."

"You might not be thankin' me when you catch up with Stewart. He's quite a handful, and he don't travel alone. You might be bitin' off more 'n you can swaller."

"I'm willin' to give it a try."

6

Lucas Cain bought a new horse to replace Charley. His new horse looked so much like Charley, that he could have been a reincarnation of his first horse. Lucas reasoned that if England could have eight kings name Henry, he could certainly have two horses named Charley, so the new horse became Charley II.

Half-way between Mascoran and Sapello, New Mexico, Lucas decided that Charley II was too new to be trusted for the long, through the desert, ride. Because he had been paralleling the railroad track, he decided to flag down the next south bound train. He had done so before, so he didn't anticipate any problem with getting aboard.

Lucas waited for the train for three hours. When first he saw it, it was approaching at about twenty miles-per-hour, a respectable enough speed, though the vastness of the landscape made it appear as if the train was going much slower. Against the great panorama of the desert the train seemed puny, and even the smoke that poured from its stack made but a tiny scar against the orange vault of sunset-sky.

He could hear the train quite easily, the sound of its puffing engine carrying to him across the wide, flat ground, the way sound travels across water. He stepped up onto the track and began waving. When he heard the steam valve close and the train begin braking, he knew that the engineer had spotted him and was going to stop. As the engine approached, it gave some perspective as to how large the desert really was, for the train that had appeared so tiny before was now a behemoth, blocking out the sky. It ground to a reluctant halt, its stack puffing black smoke, and its driver wheels wreathed in tendrils of white steam which purpled as it drifted away in the fading light.

The engineer's face appeared in the window, and Lucas felt a prickly sensation as he realized that someone was aiming a gun at him. He couldn't see the gun, but he knew that whoever it was...probably the fireman...had to be hiding in the tender.

"What do you want, mister? Why'd you stop us?" the engineer asked.

Lucas took his hat off and brushed his hair out of his eyes. The hair was lank, and grained like oak, worn trail-weary long, just over his ears. With it repositioned, he put his hat, sweat-stained and well-worn, back on his head.

"I'm afraid my horse has gone lame on me," Lucas explained. "I need a ride to the next town, and I'm willing to pay full fare."

The engineer studied him for a moment as if trying to ascertain whether or not Lucas represented any danger to him or to his passengers. Finally, he decided it would be safe to pick up this stranger.

"All right," the engineer said. "A dollar will get you to

Sapello. We'll be there in just over an hour. Take the second car."

"I see you have a stock car. For passenger's horses?"

"That'll cost you a half-dollar extra."

"Good enough, and thanks," Lucas said. He took Charley II's reins, and started toward the rear of the train. "Oh, and you can tell your fireman it's all right to come out now."

"What the hell? How did you know I was in here?" the fireman's muffled voice called.

Lucas knew because his very life often depended upon his ability to interpret such things.

The conductor climbed down from the first car after the private car.

"What's going on, here?" the conductor asked.

"I'm buying a ticket to the next town for my horse and me," Lucas answered.

"Mister, the place to do that is in a railroad depot."

Lucas made a point of looking around. "I looked around, but I didn't see one. So I figured I would just flag the train down. The engineer seemed to be all right with that."

"Yes, well it isn't the engineer's train. It's my train."

"You can take that up with the engineer. In the meantime, I'm going to pull the ramp down and get my horse into the stock car, then I'm going to board the train. If you'll come see me once I'm aboard, I'll pay the fare. Now, if you will excuse me, I think Charley II is ready to take a ride."

"All right, but don't take all day," the conductor said.

After getting Charley II loaded, Lucas boarded. There were a couple of dozen passengers in the car—men, women, and children—and they all looked up in curiosity at the man who had caused the train to stop in the middle of the desert. Lucas touched the brim of his hat, then walked to the last seat on the right and settled into it. As soon as the train got underway, the conductor came to collect the fare. Once the conductor left, Lucas pulled his legs up so that his knees were resting on the seatback in front of him, reached up and casually tipped his hat forward, then folded his arms across his chest. Within moments, he was sound asleep.

AT THE NEXT stop he was back in Sapello. After getting Charley II down from the car, Lucas rode down to the saloon, and tied his horse off out front. Once inside, he stepped up to the bar, and slapped a coin down in front of him. "How 'bout a beer?"

The sound of the coin made the saloonkeeper look around.

"Lucas Cain," the bartender said, smiling at him. "I haven't seen you since...when? Topeka?"

"Brett Taylor," Lucas said, dredging up the barkeep's name from somewhere deep in the recesses of his mind. The Topeka reference had helped.

The broadening smile on the bartender's face showed how pleased he was to be remembered by this man. Brett shoved the coin back to Lucas. "First one is on me, Lucas. Old friends who drop by always get the first one free."

"Thanks," Lucas said.

"I heard you caught up with Ed Meachum," Brett said.

"Yeah," Lucas replied without elaboration.

"Well, you did us all a favor. Meachum was a no-good, murdering son of a bitch, is what he was."

"He was that, all right," Lucas replied.

Brett was good at his job, and one of the attributes of being a good bartender was the ability to determine when a customer wanted to talk, and when a customer would rather be left alone. It quickly became obvious that Lucas just wanted to enjoy his drink in peace, so Brett slid on down to the far end of the bar and began wiping the bar.

Lucas picked up his beer, then slowly surveyed the interior of the saloon. Half a dozen tables occupied by a dozen or so men, filled the room, and tobacco smoke hovered in a noxious cloud just under the ceiling. Lucas was a rambling man, and during the past several years these kinds of surroundings had become his heritage. The saloons, cow towns, stables, dusty streets, and open prairies he had encountered had redefined him.

LUCAS WAS ONLY HALFWAY through his drink when the sheriff arrived.

"This is Lucas Cain, Sheriff," Brett said, "and this is Sheriff Jensen."

"I see you're wearing a badge. U.S. Marshal?"

"Yes."

"What are you doing in Sapello, Marshal?"

"I thought I might have supper and maybe spend a night in a real bed before going out after Stewart."

"Stewart? You mean Dudley Stewart?"

"Yes. Do you have any information on him?"

"Only that he's going to be a handful. As far as I know, he isn't anywhere around Sapello. Good heavens, you haven't heard anything that would put him here, have you?"

"No. Like I said, I just want a drink, supper, and a real bed for the night."

"Well, I hope you find everything you need in our fair town," the sheriff said. He smiled. "Except Stewart. I'd just as soon that son of a bitch stay as far away from here as he can get."

As always, Lucas limited himself to just one beer, then he found a restaurant, where he had supper. The special tonight was chicken and dumplings and when the meal arrived, Lucas felt a lump in his throat as he recalled a memory.

CAPE GIRARDEAU, MISSOURI—1869

"Close your eyes," Rosie said.

"Why do you want me to close my eyes?" Lucas replied. Lucas was sitting at the table in the dining room.

"Because you're my husband, and you're supposed to do what I say," Rosie replied with a big smile.

"Now, wait a minute. As I recall the wedding vows, you are the one who is supposed to love, honor, and *obey*," Lucas said, with emphasis on the word obey.

"Well, two out of three isn't bad," Rosie replied. "Now, please, close your eyes until I tell you to open them."

"All right," Lucas said with a little laugh. "My eyes are closed."

Lucas heard Rosie leave the dining room, then return. She put something on the table.

"All right, you can open your eyes now."

When Lucas opened his eyes, he saw that she had put a plate of chicken and dumplings before him.

"Well now, how about this?" Lucas said with a wide smile.

"I know that this meal is your favorite," Rosie said.

"That's right. I don't know why you decided to make chicken and dumplings today, but if you'd come over here, I'll give you a big hug just to tell you I love you."

"Okay, papa," Rosie said. This time her smile could almost be characterized as mysterious.

"When did you start calling me papa?"

"Well, I admit it is a little early but by my calculations, I'm about seven months too early."

"What?" Lucas shouted. "A baby? Are you sure?"

"Oh yes, I'm very sure."

Lucas stood up and pulled Rosie to him in a big embrace, topped off by a deep kiss.

"We need to be thinking about names," Lucas said. "What do you think we should name him?"

Rosie laughed. "What makes you so certain the baby will be a boy?"

"The first one will be a boy, then we can have a girl so that he'll have a little sister to look out for."

"Or she can have a little brother to boss around," Rosie said with a little laugh.

But neither scenario was to be.

When the time came, Lucas fetched the doctor, then as the doctor attended Rosie, Lucas paced back and forth in the living room. His Aunt Tillie was there with him.

When Lucas heard Rosie cry out in pain, he started toward the bedroom, but Tillie held up her hand to stop him.

"Let the doctor do his job, Lucas," she said. "You'd just be in the way."

"All right, but it sure seems to me like it's taking an awfully long time. Shouldn't the baby be here by now?"

"All we can do is wait," Tillie said.

They waited another hour, and as Rosie's cries became less and less, it became obvious that even Tillie was beginning to worry.

"What's wrong, Aunt Tillie? Does it normally take this long?"

"I don't know, I don't think so," Tillie admitted.

"If I haven't heard anything within the next five minutes, I'm, going to go in there and see what—"

Lucas's comment was interrupted by the appearance of Dr. Brandt. Lucas became even more concerned, when he saw the expression on Dr. Brandt's face.

"Doc, what is it?" he asked.

"I'm sorry, Lucas," Dr. Brandt said, with a sad shake of his head.

"You're sorry? What is it? What happened?" This time Lucas shouted the question.

"Childbed fever."

"What? What do you mean?"

"I'm afraid we lost her, Lucas. Rosie died during childbirth."

"No! My God, no!" Lucas shouted. He rushed by the doctor, into the bedroom where he saw Rosie lying on the bed, her legs spread upon a sheet stained with blood and the afterbirth. Her eyes were open, and unseeing.

"Rosie!" Lucas said, kneeling beside the bed and grasping her hand.

"The baby?" Tillie asked.

"A girl. She was stillborn," Dr. Brandt said in a voice that was quiet, and heavy with sorrow and regret.

For a moment, Lucas thought about not eating the chicken and dumplings the waitress had put on the table before him. But then, somehow he knew that Rosie would him to eat and enjoy. So thinking of Rosie, he smiled as he took the first bite.

7

Arnie Dawson was fifty-two years old, and had been driving a stagecoach for thirty years. He had started in Pennsylvania but interrupted his driving career to go to war. When the war ended, he came west and took up the reins again, now for the San Miguel County Stage Coach Company.

The stagecoach had left La Concepcion at ten o'clock that morning, and the driver was holding the six-horse team to a ground-eating trot. Dawson's normal route was the twenty-six miles from La Concepcion to Las Alamos and he made the trip three times a week.

He had watched his passengers as they boarded the coach back in La Concepcion. One of the women, young and pretty, was an army wife, enroute to join her husband, a lieutenant newly assigned to Fort Baker, which was just outside Las Alamos. The other woman was a mother, traveling with her two children, a boy of nine and a girl of seven. There was a farmer, a travel-wise drummer, and Lou Preston, a bank clerk who was carrying the bank pouch and would be returning with receipt for a money transfer from the bank in La Concepcion to the bank in Las Alamos.

The eight-hundred-dollar money transfer was the only thing that made this trip different from a routine run. It wasn't the first time he had carried money, but he was always a little uneasy when having to do so.

TWO MILES ahead of the stage coach, six men were waiting for the coach. The leader of the group, a man named Dudley Stewart, had a bulging left eye, which also tended to wander. He and the men who followed him, Sam Coker, Carl Mathis, Dan Dobbins, Scooter Thompson, and Hoot Calhoun, were waiting for the coach.

"You're sure there's money on this coach?" Mathis asked. "Most of the time this coach don't carry nothin'."

"It cost me twenty dollars to find out there's money being carried on this run," Stewart said. "If the feller lied to me, I'll get the money back, with interest," he added with an evil smile.

"How much money?" Thompson asked.

"I don't know how much. But it's a bank transfer, so it's going to be more than I paid to find out about it."

"How long do you think before it gets here?" Mathis asked.

Stewart chuckled. "Why? Do you have something other than this that you need to be doing?"

"He's goin' to lie 'n tell us he's got a woman waitin' on 'im," Dobbins said, and the others laughed.

"Hell, if we get the money, we all got us a woman waitin', don't we?" Coker said. "I mean, even Mathis can get 'im a whore."

"Yeah, but he has to pay extra, on account of he's so

ugly," Calhoun said. His comment was also met with laughter.

"Quit messin' around, 'n start payin' attention," Stewart said. "The coach will be here pretty soon."

WHEN THE COACH was just over half way to their destination, Dawson slowed the team from a trot to a walk to give the horses a little break.

"You think maybe the horses could trot all the way?" Clem Peters asked. Peters was the shotgun guard. Normally Dawson made the trip without a guard, but anytime there was a money shipment, there was a guard. Dawson had pointed out that the presence of a guard just announced that they were carrying money, but the banks insisted on it.

"I don't know, they might be able to, but why make 'em do it? It's easy enough to keep to the schedule without wearing them out."

"ARE YOU MARRIED TO A SOLDIER?" Teddy Raney asked the young woman who was sitting just across from him.

"I am, indeed," Claire Mason answered with a pretty smile.

"I'm going to be a soldier when I grow up," Teddy said.

"Oh, and I bet you'll a good one, too," Claire replied.

"Is your husband a general?"

Claire laughed. "No, I'm afraid he's only a lieutenant."

"I'm going to be a general."

"My, that's quite an ambition to aspire to."

"I'll be able to boss your husband around."

"I'm sure you will."

"Teddy, will you quit bothering the nice young lady?" Teddy's mother said. "I'm sorry Mrs. Mason."

"Oh, heavens, he's not bothering me at all," Claire said.

"Well, as long as he's not—" Mrs. Raney's comment was interrupted by the roar of a shotgun blast.

"Oh, heavens, what is happening?" Claire asked.

DAWSON SAW six men gathered in the road in front of the coach. One of them had just fired off a shotgun blast. The other men were holding guns, pointed at Dawson and Peters.

"Damn," Peters said.

"Don't try 'n be a hero, Clem. They's too many of 'em," Dawson warned.

"I don't intend to," Peters replied.

Suddenly, and without one word being spoken by the men who had stopped the coach, they all fired their pistols. Dawson and Peters were both hit. Peters fell from the coach, and Dawson fell into the footwell.

Stewart rode back to the door of the coach and called out to the passengers inside.

"All right, all of you climb out of the coach, now."

The passengers, with fear reflected on their faces, left the coach as ordered. They stood alongside the coach with their hands in the air.

"Which one of you is the bank clerk?" Stewart asked.

"He is," the drummer said, pointing to Preston.

"Crawl back in there and throw the pouch out," Stewart demanded.

"I…I…I," Preston said, shaking with fear, and mesmerized by Stewart's bulging eye.

"Hey, Stewart, you better let me get it," Coker said. "That little feller's 'bout to wet his pants."

"All right, hold on for just a minute 'till we take care of business," Stewart replied. He shot the banker, then the others began shooting.

"All right, Coker, get the money, and let's get out of here," Stewart ordered after the guns fell silent.

A moment later, with Stewart holding on to the bank pouch, the five men left the scene at a gallop. Behind them the shotgun guard, and every coach passenger, including the two women and the two children, lay dead in the road beside the coach.

The only one who wasn't dead, was the driver, who lay in the footwell, wounded but alive. He had heard the outlaws calling each other by name, and he was determined to stay alive long enough to tell the names.

"EIGHT HUNDRED DOLLARS?" Calhoun said in disgust, when they examined the pouch. "That's all there was?"

"Damn, it was hardly worth it," Dobbins said.

"Money is money," Coker said.

"It's not very damn much money," Dobbins said. "I mean, we killed how many people for this?"

"What difference does it make, how many we killed?" Stewart said. "It's like Coker said, money is money. And if you don't want your share, I'll divide it among the rest of us."

"No, no, I want my share," Dobbins said, quickly.

Stewart gave a snorting chuckle. "Yeah, I thought you might."

JIM YARBOROUGH WAS RIDING from La Concepcion to Las Alamos when he saw the coach stopped in the road ahead. It was very unusual to see a coach stopped like this, and he wondered what was wrong. He urged his horse into a trot.

Yarborough knew the driver, and if Dawson was having a problem with the coach, he would do what he could to help. At the very least, he could ride on ahead to send help back.

When he reached the coach he saw Dawson sitting on the driver's seat, slumped forward as if asleep.

"Arnie, what's goin' on?" Yarborough called.

"They're dead," Dawson answered in a strained voice. "They're all dead."

"Who's—" Yarborough started to say, but that's when he saw the bodies lying on the ground on the other side of the coach. "Oh, God in heaven, what happened?"

"It was Stewart," Dawson said in a strained voice.

"I've got to get you to town," Yarborough said. "I'll tie my horse on behind and I'll drive the stage."

"Don't," Dawson said.

"Don't get you to town? Arnie, there's no way I'm going to leave you out here."

"Don't leave them," Dawson said, pointing to the bodies on the side of the road.

"All right."

It took Yarborough a lot of hard work, but he managed to get all the bodies back into the coach. They were all piled on top of one another, but he knew that wouldn't matter.

It took two more hours to reach Las Alamos and the arrival in town brought a lot of curious stares. They knew this wasn't the normal driver, and why was there a horse tied on back?

Yarborough stopped in front of the stage depot because it had a big sign out front and was easy to find. A hostler came to change the team.

"Arnie's been shot," Yarborough said. "We need to get him to the doctor right away."

"What? What happened?"

"Stewart and his men held up the coach. The coach is filled with bodies."

Fifteen minutes after the coach arrived in town, Sheriff Kingsly was in the doctor's office, listening to Arnie Dawson's tale of what happened. Dawson died that very night.

THE SIGN on the road leading into town identified it as Bernal. As he did when arriving in any town, the first thing Lucas did was stop at the office of the local constabulary, be it a sheriff or a city marshal.

The sheriff was standing with his back to the door when Lucas entered.

"I'll be with you in a second," the sheriff said, as he poured himself a cup of coffee. That done, he turned around, holding the cup.

"What can I do...wait a minute, are you a US Marshal?"

"Yes."

"What are you doing here in Bernal?"

"Right now, I'm after Dudley Stewart. I don't suppose you have any idea where Stewart is, do you?"

"I don't have any idea. The only thing I know for sure, is that he isn't anywhere around here, and he has a pretty good reward on him, so I expect somebody will be out lookin' for him."

"That would be me," Lucas said.

"But you're a marshal. How come you expect to collect a reward?"

"Because I serve as a deputy U.S. Marshal without pay. That leaves me eligible to collect any bounty that has been posted. In the meantime, the marshal's badge gives me authority that is universal."

"I can see how the badge might help. What about Emil Bateman? Are you going after him?"

"Emil Bateman? No, who is he? I've never heard of him."

"He was in prison, but the son of a bitch escaped. Here, read this."

The sheriff handed Lucas a newspaper.

A Crime Most Foul

On Friday last, Emil Bateman escaped from the Territorial Prison in Santa Fe. He killed a guard in the escape, but this wasn't the end of his perfidious activity. Jason Harrison, owner of the Harrison Trading Emporium was killed on the same day that Bateman escaped, and while there is no evidence to support the charge that he was killed by Bateman, there is room for the belief that he did so.

But it was after he left Harrison's Trading Emporium, if indeed Bateman was guilty of that crime, that his most heinous acts were undertaken. Bateman stopped at the Colby Farm where he killed Mr. Wes Colby, his wife, Elaine Colby, and his son Lonnie.

Not content with the evil he had already visited upon the Colby family, he turned to the fifteen-year-old daughter, committing the vilest attack on her. Miss Colby survived the attack and, though grievously wounded, was able to make it into town where she reported the horrendous incident to the authorities.

"Damn gruesome," Lucas said after reading the article and returning the newspaper to the sheriff.

"There is a reward out for him, not as big as the one for Stewart, but five hundred dollars isn't something you would just turn your back on."

"No, it isn't," Lucas agreed.

"You'll go after him?"

"Yeah, I'll get started tomorrow."

8

Fifteen miles north of where Lucas was spending the night, Emil Bateman rode into the town of Pecos. This was the first town he had been in since he broke out of prison. He looked around cautiously, but then he was cautious everywhere he went now, because the least mistake could put him back in prison.

He stopped at the Brown Dirt Saloon, where he planned to have his first drink in two years. There was a drunk passed out on the steps in front of the place and Bateman had to step over him in order to go inside.

Because all the chimneys of all the lanterns were soot-covered, what light there was, was dingy and filtered through drifting smoke. The place smelled of whiskey, stale beer, and tobacco smoke. There was a long bar on the left, with dirty towels hanging on hooks about every five feet along its front. A large mirror was behind the bar, but like everything else about the saloon, it was so dirty that Bateman could scarcely see any images in it, and what he could see was distorted by imperfections in the glass.

Over against the back wall, near the foot of the stairs, a cigar-scarred, beer-stained upright piano was being played by a bald-headed musician. One of the saloon girls stood alongside, swaying to the music.

"What'll it be?" the bartender asked.

"Whiskey. And leave the bottle," Bateman said.

"Mister, you sound like a serious drinker. All I ask is that you don't get drunk and cause no trouble."

"I asked for whiskey, not a damn lecture," Bateman said, sharply.

"All right, all right, I was just commentin' is all," the bartender said.

When the bottle of whiskey was put before him, one of the percentage girls came up to him, greeting him with a practiced smile.

"Surely a handsome man like you doesn't plan to drink alone, do you?" she asked.

Bateman checked his image in the mirror. He had a misshapen nose, bulging eyes, and a weak chin. He chuckled.

"Honey, if you think I'm handsome, you need to get your eyes checked. But I'll buy you a drink, then maybe we can go upstairs together. You won't fight me, will you?"

"Not if you pay me."

Bateman laughed. "You do get right to the point though, don't you?"

"There's no reason not to."

"All right, you just got yourself a customer."

A SLIGHT BREEZE filled the muslin curtains and lifted them out over the wide-planked floor of the hotel. Lucas moved to the window and looked out over the town, which was just beginning to awaken. Water was being heated behind the laundry and boxes were being stacked behind the grocery store. A team of four big horses pulled a fully loaded freight wagon down the main street.

From somewhere, Lucas could smell bacon frying and his stomach growled, reminding him that he was hungry. He splashed some water in the basin, washed his face and hands, then put on his hat and went downstairs. There were a couple of people in the lobby, one napping in one of the chairs, the other reading a newspaper. Neither of them paid any attention to Lucas as he left the hotel.

The morning sun was bright, but not yet hot. The sky was clear and the air was crisp. As he walked toward the café, he heard sounds of commerce: the ring of a blacksmith's hammer, a carpenter's saw, and the rattle of working wagons. That was as opposed to last night's sounds of liquor bottles, an off-key piano, laughter, and boisterous conversations. How different the tenor of a town was between the business of morning, and the play of evening.

Half an hour later, Lucas was enjoying a breakfast of bacon, eggs, fried potatoes, biscuits and gravy when a boy of about sixteen came to his table.

"You are Marshal Cain?"

"Yes."

"The sheriff, he wants to see you."

"All right. You tell him I'll be down soon as I finish my breakfast."

The boy nodded. "I will do so." He turned to leave.

"Wait," Lucas called out. When the boy turned back to him, Lucas gave him a quarter.

"For bringing me the message," Lucas said.

"The boy smiled. "Thank you, sir!" he said.

THE SHERIFF LOOKED up when Lucas stepped into the office. "I see that Davy gave you the message."

"Yes, he did. What's going on?"

"I've got a lead on where Bateman might be."

"Good. Where would that be?"

"It's a town called Pecos. It's about fifteen miles southeast of here if you're interested."

"Thanks for the information. I don't think I got your name."

"It's Spencer—Bud Spencer."

Lucas nodded his head. "I'll remember you if I get Bateman."

AS LUCAS RODE out of Bernal, he wondered what he would find in front of him. He had never been to Pecos, but he was pretty sure he would be able describe it.

It was about a three-hour ride, and the town was just as Lucas had pictured it, a single street, lined on both sides by the businesses of the town. Most of the buildings were of adobe construction, but two were of wood and one, the bank, was constructed of brick. One of the wooden buildings was a saloon. Like saloons Lucas had seen all over the West, it had a high, false-front with the name painted in black letters, outlined in red.

Lucas was hungry and thirsty, but the long, hot ride made him more thirsty than hungry. Dismounting in front, he tied off his horse, then pushed through the swinging bat-wing doors to step inside.

The bartender moved down to confront him.

"What'll you have?"

"Beer."

The bartender drew a mug from the beer barrel and put it on the bar before him.

Lucas showed the bartender his badge. "I'm told Emil Bateman was seen in here yesterday."

"I suppose he was. I'd never seen him before, so I can't swear that he was here, but there were a couple of men in here who swear that it was him."

"Is he still here?"

"I don't know. He might still be in town, but he's not here in the saloon."

LUCAS CHECKED in with the city marshal.

"Someone said he was in town," Marshal Gibson said, "but I've been checkin' and nobody but one man says he seen him."

"Well, I guess I'm at a dead end then," Lucas said.

"I heard what he did to that little girl and her family. I sure as hell hope somebody can find him."

"Yeah, I do, too, and not just for the reward."

BATEMAN WAS HAVING lunch in the Good Eats Café in Pecos. He had planned to leave earlier, but he was late getting started. He decided it wouldn't hurt to get another meal before he moved on. He chose a table back in the corner which got him some separation from the other diners, and it was in shadows.

"I understand his name is Lucas Cain," he heard someone say.

"Who's Lucas Cain?"

"A US Marshal."

"I sure as hell hope he's come here to look for that Bateman fella. You know, the one what raped that little girl after he kilt her mama 'n daddy, 'n her brother?"

"Yeah, I hope so, too. Clyde Tipsword said he seen 'im down at the Brown Dirt. You might 'member that Tipsword was in prison, 'n he know'd Bateman whilst he was in there."

"So, Tipsword told on Bateman, did he?"

"Yeah. Well, you know there's a reward out for Bateman, 'n I'm a' thinkin' that Tipsword's plannin' on gettin' some of it for tellin' that he seen Bateman."

"I ain't never seen Marshal Cain before. What's he look like?"

"He's a tall man, got broad shoulders, brown hair. Oh, and he's wearin' a red shirt. I just seen 'im over at El Lobo's."

"Is he still there?"

"I expect he is. It was just before I come in here. I reckon he's eatin' his dinner."

Bateman listened to every word the two men said. He remembered Tipsword, and he remembered that he was the kind of prisoner who ratted on the others to get better treatment for himself. And it was that, his willingness to squeal on the others, that had earned him an early parole.

If Tipsword was still in town, Bateman planned to settle accounts with him. But first, he had Lucas Cain to deal with.

Leaving the Good Eats, Bateman walked down the street to El Lobo's. A quick glance through the window located Cain, or at least the man Bateman had heard described.

Bateman stepped in between El Lobo's and the Ladies' Goods store next door. He pulled his pistol, held it down by his side, and waited.

INSIDE EL LOBO'S, Lucas stood at the counter to pay for his food.

"I hope you enjoyed your meal, Marshal," the cashier said.

"It was very good."

"I'm glad you liked it. And I hope you find Bateman."

"You've heard about that, have you?"

"Oh, heavens, by now, I expect everyone in town knows that you're goin' after him."

"Yeah, including Bateman. I'm sure he's left town by now."

As soon as Lucas stepped outside, Bateman called out to him.

"Cain!"

Lucas didn't recognize the voice, but he did recognize the tone. It wasn't a greeting—it was a challenge. He threw himself down in the street, below the porch, drawing his gun as he did so.

Bateman pulled the trigger at the same time he gave the shout, but Lucas' quick reaction got him out of the line of fire. Lucas returned fire.

Bateman's bullet missed. Lucas' didn't.

The gunplay attracted the attention of many of the townspeople, and their first reaction was to jump back out of the way. But when no more gunshots sounded, they began to come out in a curious exploration of what had just happened.

They saw Lucas Cain standing near the opening between El Lobo's and the Ladies' Goods store. He was holding a gun in his hand and looking down at a body that lay on the ground.

The City Marshal came hurrying through the townspeople who were now gathering around the scene. "What happened here?" Gibson asked.

"Someone shot at me, I shot back," Lucas said.

Gibson turned the body over for a closer examination. He smiled. "Marshal Cain, I would say you've just made a five-hundred-dollar shot. This here is Emil Bateman."

"Good riddance," one of the townspeople said.

After remaining in town long enough to collect the reward, Lucas left to continue the hunt for Dudley Stewart. He spent the next six weeks following every lead, without success. Then, at a remote trading post in Santa Fe County, Lucas learned that Stewart and a man named Scooter Thompson who rode with him, might be in the town of El Pueblo.

9

After six hours on a bumping, rattling, jerking, and dusty stagecoach, the passengers' first view of El Pueblo was often a bitter disappointment. Sometimes visitors from the East had to have the town pointed out to them, for from this perspective, and at this distance, the settlement looked little more inviting than another group of the brown hummocks and hills common to this country.

LUCAS STOPPED on a ridge just above the road leading into El Pueblo. He took a swallow from his canteen and watched the stage as it started down from the pass, into the town. Then, corking the canteen, he slapped his legs against the side of his horse and loped down the long ridge. Although he was farther away from town than the coach, he would beat it there, because he was going by a more direct route.

Lucas saw a small sign just on the edge of town.

El Pueblo
population 294
A growing community.

The weathered board and faded letters of the sign indicated that it had been there for some time. Lucas doubted El Pueblo was a growing community.

As Lucas rode into El Pueblo, he surveyed the little town closely. In addition to the false-fronted shanties that lined each side of the street, there were a few adobe buildings, and even some tents, straggling along for nearly a quarter of a mile. Then, just as abruptly as the town started, it quit, and the prairie began again.

In the winter and spring, the street was a muddy mire worked by the horse's hooves and mixed with their droppings, so that it became a stinking, sucking, pool of ooze. But it was summer now, early afternoon, and the sun was yellow and hot. Dismounting in front of the saloon, Lucas checked the pistol in his holster and pushed through the batwing doors.

The shadows made the saloon seem cooler inside, but that was illusory. It was nearly as hot inside as out, and without the benefit of a breath of air it was even more stifling. The customers were sweating in their drinks and wiping their faces with bandanas.

As always when he entered a strange saloon, Lucas checked the place out. To one unfamiliar with what he was doing, Lucas's glance appeared to be little more than idle curiosity. But it was a studied surveillance. Who was armed? What type guns were they carrying? How were they wearing them? Was there anyone here he knew? More importantly, was there anyone here who would know him, and who might take this opportunity to settle some old score, real or imagined, for himself or a friend, or even try to make a name for himself by killing Lucas.

It appeared that there were only workers and drifters here. The couple of men who were armed were young men, probably wearing their guns as much for show as anything. And from the way the pistols rode on their hips, Lucas would have bet that they had never used them for anything but target practice, and not very successfully at that.

The bartender stood behind the bar. In front of him were two glasses with whiskey remaining in them, and he poured the whiskey back into a bottle, corked it, and put the bottle on the shelf behind the bar. He wiped the glasses out with his stained apron, then set them among the unused glasses. Seeing Lucas step up to the bar, the bartender moved down toward him.

"Beer," Lucas said.

The barman reached for an empty mug that was setting on the bar.

"In a clean glass," Lucas added.

Shrugging, the saloonkeeper pulled a glass from beneath the bar.

"I'm looking for two men," Lucas said.

"Mister, if you want whiskey or beer, I'm your man. If you want anything else, I can't help you," the bartender replied.

"One of the men has a bad eye that you can't miss. It bulges and tends to wander around."

"I told you, Mister. What I do is pour drinks. Other than that, I mind my own business."

"They are murdering scum," Lucas said.

"You the law?"

Lucas wasn't wearing his badge, but he took it out and showed it to the bartender.

"I'm a deputy U.S. Marshal," he said, "and if I can find them here, it's worth five dollars to me."

The saloon owner said nothing, but he raised his head and looked toward the stairs at the back of the room.

"Thanks," Lucas said, sliding a five-dollar bill across the bar.

At the back of the saloon, a flight of wooden stairs led up to an enclosed loft. Lucas guessed that the two doors at the head of the stairs led to the rooms used by the prostitutes who worked in the saloon. He started to pull his gun, then thought better of it, and slipped out his knife instead.

The few men in the saloon had been talking and laughing among themselves. When they saw Lucas pull his knife, their conversation died, and they watched him walk quietly up the steps.

"I don't know who that feller is after, but I'm glad it ain't me," one of the saloon patrons said.

From the rooms above him, Lucas could hear muffled sounds that left little doubt as to what was going on behind the closed doors. Normally such sounds called forth ribald comments from the patrons below, but now there was no teasing whatever; everyone knew that a life-and-death confrontation was about to take place. No one knew why, but then such things occurred often, and no one really cared about the reasons.

Lucas tried to open the first door, but it was locked. He knocked on it.

"Go 'way, Stewart," a man's voice called from the other side of the door. "You've had your woman, now let me have mine."

Go 'way, Stewart, he said. That meant Stewart was in the other room.

Lucas moved to the next door, raised his foot, then kicked it hard. The door flew open with a crash and the woman inside the room screamed.

"What the hell?" the man shouted. He stood up quickly, and Lucas saw with a sinking feeling that it wasn't Stewart. He heard a crash of glass from the next room and he dashed to the window and looked down. He saw Stewart just getting to his feet from the leap to the alley below.

Damn! He'd been suckered in by an old trick. Dudley Stewart had deliberately used his own name when he said go away, in order to throw Lucas off. Lucas kicked out the window and started to climb onto the sill to go after Stewart.

"You sonofabitch! Who the hell are you?" Scooter Thompson shouted. Out of the corner of his eye, Lucas saw Thompson coming after him with a knife. The outlaw lunged toward Lucas, making a long, would-be, stomach opening swipe. Lucas barely managed to avoid the point of the knife. One inch closer and he would have been disemboweled.

"I'll cut you open like a pig, you sonofabitch," Thompson growled. "Who the hell you think you are bustin' in like this?"

Thompson swung again and Lucas jumped deftly to one side, then counter-thrust. The blade of Lucas's knife buried itself in Thompson's neck, and Lucas felt hot blood spilling across his hand. The man gurgled, and his eyes bulged open wide. Then, slowly, he slipped to the floor.

"Dudley Stewart," Lucas said, kneeling beside the wounded man. "Where is he heading?"

"Who...who are you?" Thompson asked. Blood bubbled at his lips when he spoke.

"The name is Cain. Lucas Cain."

"I ain't never even heard of you."

"Where is Dudley Stewart?" Lucas asked again.

"I reckon you'll just have to keep lookin' for him," Thompson said, dying with the laughter from hell on his lips.

Lucas looked over at the woman who was standing there, holding the sheet over her naked body, shocked into silence.

"Are you all right, Miss?"

The woman didn't speak, but nodded.

"I'll get somebody up here to take care of this," Lucas said, indicating the body that was now lying in a pool of its own blood.

"I DON'T PARTICULARLY like it when somebody gets killed in my town," Marshal Pitts said, "but, if you're going after Stewart, well, more power to you."

"Stewart was here in town," Lucas said. "You had your chance to get him."

"I don't know that he was here," Marshal Pitts replied.

"He was here, all right. I just missed him."

"And who is this man you killed?"

"From descriptions I have read of him, I believe it's Scooter Thompson."

"Any reward on him?"

"One hundred dollars."

"If this is who you say he is."

"Don't you have any reward posters?"

"Yeah, I do."

"Find one for Scooter Thompson. It has a drawing of him, and a description."

Marshall Pitts found the reward posters for Scooter Thompson and Dudley Stewart. Then, after visiting with the bartender and the two prostitutes, he was convinced that Stewart had, in fact, been in his town. He was also convinced that Thompson was who Lucas said he was, so he gave Lucas a statement verifying receipt of the corpse of one Scooter Thompson. He would have to get a judge to sign off on it before he could collect the one-hundred-dollar reward, but it was something Lucas had done many times.

IT HAD BEEN two weeks since Stewart had managed to escape the US Marshal who was coming for him. He knew, now, that Scooter Thompson had been killed, but he felt no particular sense of regret. His only thought was that Thompson had made it possible for him to escape.

Now Stewart was ready for his next job, and he had gathered the others—Sam Coker, Carl Mathis, Dan Dobbins, and Hoot Calhoun—to plan the operation.

"Just how much money do you reckon that bank will have?" Dobbins asked, after hearing Stewart lay out his plans for a bank robbery. "I mean we didn't get that much money off the stage coach that we robbed. I'm hopin' this is a little better."

"What do you mean, how much money will it have? It's a bank," Stewart answered. "Banks have money, that's why they are there."

"Yeah, Dan, it ain't like we're robbin' a grocery store," Sam Coker said.

"I was just wonderin' is all."

"Don't wonder," Stewart said. "Just do what I tell you,

and we'll all come out with more money than we've ever had before."

Dobbins chuckled. "Well, hell, it won't take a hell of a lot of money for it to be more 'n I've ever had."

"Where did you say this bank was?" Mathis asked.

"It's in Dos Nachos," Stewart answered. "It should be easy enough to take. There's only one city marshal, and it's mostly farmers that live around the town, and there don't hardly none of 'em carry a gun."

"When do we go?" Calhoun asked.

Stewart smiled. "Tomorrow."

LUCAS WAS HAVING a beer in the Saddle and Spur Saloon in the little town of Ortiz. He had lost all trail of Dudley Stewart, and now had no choice but to visit saloons in small towns and start asking questions. The Saddle and Spur had been as unproductive as the last three had been. Despite that, he hadn't given up yet. A man like Stewart wasn't going to stay quiet for too long.

"You want some company, *Señor*?" a woman asked, approaching him from the opposite end of the bar.

"Might as well," Lucas answered. "Give the lady a drink," he said to the bartender.

"Haven't seen you before," the bar girl said.

"I'd be surprised if you had, since this is the first time I've ever been here."

"My name is Juanita."

"I'm Lucas."

As the two talked, Lucas realized that she wanted him to take her upstairs, but he avoided that by buying her more drinks. As he continued to buy her drinks and engage her in conversation, it became evident that she would rather earn her money by friendly conversation than by lying on her back.

Neither of the two noticed the big man, with a scowl on his face, leave the saloon.

After another few minutes of visiting, Lucas told Juanita that he had to leave. She followed him to the door.

Lucas had just stepped out into the street when he heard Juanita yell.

"*Señor* Lucas, look out!"

Lucas felt a blow to the side of his head. The warning hadn't prevented the attack, but it did allow him to keep his feet.

"I'm goin' to whip your ass, you sumbitch!" the man who attacked him said. He swung wildly, but Lucas slipped the punch easily, then counter punched with a quick, slashing left to his attacker's face. It was a good, well-connected blow, but the man just flinched once, then laughed a low, evil laugh.

"Five dollars says Mooney whups him," Lucas heard someone say. "Look how much bigger he is."

"I don't know, I've seen men who were smaller than the other guy fight before. They ain't all that big, but they're tough as rawhide."

With an angry roar, Mooney rushed Lucas again, and Lucas stepped aside, avoiding him like a matador side-stepping a charging bull. And, like a charging bull, Mooney slammed into a hitching rail, smashing through it as if it were kindling. He turned and faced Lucas again.

Nearly everyone who had been in the saloon had come outside by now, and they were watching the fight with a great deal of interest. They knew it would be a test of quickness and agility against brute strength, and they wanted to see if the stranger could handle Mooney.

Lucas and Mooney circled around for a moment, holding their fists doubled in front of them, each trying to test the mettle of the other.

Mooney swung, a club-like swing which Lucas leaned away from. Lucas counter punched and again he scored well, but again, Mooney laughed it off. As the fight went on, it developed that Lucas could hit Mooney at will, and though Mooney laughed off his early blows, it was soon obvious that there was a cumulative effect to Lucas's punches. Both of Mooney's eyes began to puff up, and there was a nasty cut on his lip. Then Lucas caught Mooney in the nose with a long left, and when he felt the nose go under his hand, he knew that he had broken it.

The bridge of his nose exploded like a smashed tomato and started bleeding profusely. The blood ran across Mooney's teeth and chin.

Lucas looked for another chance at the nose, but Mooney started protecting it. Lucas was unable to get it again, though the fact that Mooney was favoring it told Lucas that the nose was hurting him.

Except for the opening blow, Mooney hadn't connected. The big man was throwing great swinging blows toward Lucas, barely missing him on a couple of occasions, but as yet, none of them had connected.

After four or five such swinging blows, Lucas noticed that Mooney was leaving a slight opening for a good right punch, if he could just slip it across his shoulder. He waited, and on Mooney's next swing, Lucas threw a solid right, straight at the place where he thought Mooney's nose would be. He timed it perfectly and had the satisfaction of hearing a bellow of pain from Mooney for the first time.

Mooney was obviously growing more tired now, and

he began charging more and swinging less. Lucas got set for one of his charges, then as Mooney rushed by with his head down, Lucas stepped to one side. Like a matador thrusting his sword into the bull in a killing lunge, Lucas sent a powerful right jab to Mooney's jaw. Mooney went down. He got up on his hands and knees, and Lucas was waiting for him to stand up, but Mooney just stayed there. He shook his head.

"I've had enough, Mister, I ain't goin' to fight no more."

"Why did you start this fight?" Lucas asked.

"Because Juanita would drink with you, but she wouldn't drink with me."

"If you would behave yourself, *Señor* Mooney, I would drink with you," Juanita said.

10

There wasn't much going on in Dos Nachos. Sun-baked buildings lined each side of Center Street. A wagon rolled slowly out of town, the farmer and his wife sitting together on the driver's seat. There were two small boys playing together in the back of the wagon, which held the purchases for which they had come to town.

On the porch of the Malone Mercantile, an old black and white dog slept, uninterested in a brown cat that was sleeping not ten feet away. At the back of the porch, sitting in the shade of the building, two old men with white hair and beards, faced each other over a checker game. In the school yard, boys and girls were playing at recess under the watchful eyes of their teacher, Miss Margrabe. The ringing of a blacksmith's hammer could be heard all up and down Center Street.

The peaceful appearance of the town belied the drama that was playing out in the Cattlemen and Farmers' Bank. At that very moment, Sherwood Patterson, the bank owner, was standing against the wall with three of the townspeople who had come into the bank to do business. Patterson and the three citizens had their hands raised as they looked on with fear at the five men who were robbing the bank.

The leader of the outlaws was Dudley Stewart. Stewart was so sure of himself that he wasn't even wearing a mask. The lack of a face mask exposed that the left side of his face was disfigured by a bulging eyeball. Carl Mathis, Dan Dobbins, Sam Coker, and Hoot Calhoun, also unmasked, were the men who made up the Stewart gang. At the moment, Stewart was holding his pistol against the head of the single bank teller, who was kneeling in front of the safe, turning the combination.

"Hurry up," Stewart ordered.

"I...I'm trying," Thurman Burns said. "But I'm so scared I keep making mistakes."

Stewart put the barrel of his pistol against Burns' temple. "Make another mistake, and your brains will be scattered all over this safe."

"All right, all right," Burns said as he cleared the combination and started over.

OUTSIDE THE BANK, Dan Rafferty, who was just arriving to cash a bank draft, happened to look through the window before going into the bank. He couldn't see Stewart or the bank teller, but he did see the bank president and the three bank patrons who were standing against the wall with their hands up.

Rafferty ran down the street, then dashed into the sheriff's office. "Sheriff! Sheriff! The bank's bein' robbed!"

Sheriff Delmer Hamby jumped from his chair so fast

that it turned over. Reaching for the gun rack behind him, he grabbed a Henry rifle.

"Come on, we've got to stop them," Hamby shouted.

"We? What do you mean, we? You're the sheriff. I told you what was happenin', 'n that's good enough," Rafferty said.

"All right, but you can at least sound the alarm, can't you?"

"The alarm, yeah," Rafferty said, and leaving the sheriff's office at the same time as Hamby, he went two buildings farther down to the fire station and began clanging the fire alarm bell.

The sound of the bell alerted the town.

BACK IN THE BANK, Burns gave a little sigh of relief as the door came open.

"Coker, get the sack over here," Stewart ordered.

"Now, put all the money in the sack," Stewart said when Coker held the cloth bag out.

Working quickly but with shaking hands, Burns put all the money from the safe into the bag.

"Well, that's more like it," Stewart said. He pulled the trigger, and as blood gushed from the exit wound of the bullet, Burns fell forward, half in and half out of the open safe.

By now the bell was ringing and the outlaws heard it.

"Damn, they's a fire some 'ers," Calhoun said.

"Fire hell," Stewart said. "That's for us!"

Stewart looked toward Calhoun, Mathis, and Dobbins, who were holding their guns on Patterson and the three bank patrons, one of whom was a woman.

"Take care of 'em," Stewart said.

Mathis and Dobbins opened fire and with cries of alarm and pain, the four who were being held, fell to the floor.

As word of the bank robbery spread through the town, wagons were brought out and placed at each end of the street to block off their escape. A dozen of the town's citizens were armed and waiting behind the two barricades.

The front door of the bank opened, and the five men hurried out, one of them carrying a stuffed bag. They started toward their horses, which were tied to the hitch rail.

"Hold it right there, Stewart! You ain't goin' nowhere!" Sheriff Hamby called. Hamby recognized Stewart because of the drawing and description of him on a reward poster that was on the wall in his office.

"We need to get out of here!" Stewart called.

Hamby took a shot, his bullet whizzing by Stewart's head.

One of the other citizens of the town, let go with a blast from his shotgun. He didn't hit anyone, but the front window of the bank came crashing down.

The bank robbers mounted, then galloped down the street, now being fired on by several of the town's citizens. They were firing wildly as they fled the bank.

"Dudley, I'm hit, I'm hit!" Dobbins called, as he tumbled from his horse. Next to go down was Mathis.

"Don't leave us!" Mathis shouted as Stewart, Coker, and Calhoun galloped away.

When they reached the end of the street, their way

was blocked by a wagon barricade that was manned by half a dozen townsmen.

"Damn!" Stewart shouted.

The three remaining bank robbers jerked their horses around and galloped down to the opposite end of the street where they encountered another blockade.

"This way!" Stewart shouted, and he led the other two through the school yard which was still filled with school children and Miss Margrabe.

"Hold your fire, hold your fire!" Sheriff Hamby shouted. "You might hit one of the kids!"

When Stewart and his two men got to the opposite side of the school yard, they turned and fired at the kids, realizing that the townspeople would stop to tend the kids, rather than chase after them.

In frustration and anger, the townspeople ran through the school yard then formed a skirmish line to shoot at the cloud of dust raised by the retreating outlaws.

"Hold your fire!" Sheriff Hamby called. "They're out of range—you're just wasting ammunition."

"What the hell, Sheriff, you ain't just goin' to let 'em get away, are you?" Jed Sikes called out in frustration.

"No, we'll go after them," Hamby said, looking back toward the street where he saw that some of the townsmen were holding Dobbins and Mathis captive. "In the meantime, we've got two of 'em."

"Yeah, and they got some of us," Sikes said. "Look."

Sikes pointed to the schoolyard, where a little girl and Miss Margrabe were down. The rest of the children were gathered around them, some of them crying.

"Oh, my God," Hamby said reverently.

"Let's hang 'em! Let's hang the bastards!" somebody shouted, pointing to the two captives.

"I'll get the rope!" another said.

Several of the citizens of the town started toward Dobbins and Mathis.

"Hold it, hold it!" Hamby shouted, and he shot into the air. "There will be no lynching while I'm sheriff, and if you try it, I'll kill you, or you'll have to kill me."

"What are you tellin' us, Sheriff? Are you sayin' these two murderers aren't goin' to hang?"

"No, I'm not telling you that. They're going to hang, all right, but it's going to be legal. We're going to try 'em today, find 'em guilty, then hang 'em as soon as we can get gallows built. Now, somebody get a doctor for Miss Margrabe and this little girl."

"We don't need a doctor for either one of 'em, Sheriff. It's too late for that," someone said.

THREE DAYS LATER, a mass funeral was held for the seven who were killed—Sherwood Patterson, president of the bank, Thurman Burns, the teller, Calib Griffin, Harry Lee, and Martha Tilden, who were killed in the bank, plus nine-year-old Emma Lou Grant and the teacher, Loretta Margrabe, who were killed on the school ground. Miss Margrabe had no relatives in town, but she had made several friends, so she wasn't without mourners. It was said that the crowd that gathered in the cemetery for the burying was the largest crowd ever to gather in the small town of Dos Nachos.

LUCAS CAIN, having heard of the robbery and murder, arrived in Dos Nachos on the day of the funeral. He stopped at the Horse Shoe Saloon, tied Charley II to the hitching rail, then went inside. Seeing that he was the only customer, he looked around in surprise.

"Are you open? Where is everyone?"

"Ain't you heard?" the bartender asked. "They're all at the cemetery buryin' our dead. We had a bank robbery 'n shootin' here last Monday, 'n seven of our own got kilt."

"Yes, I had heard that," Lucas said. "I just didn't realize that I was arriving on the same day as the funerals. It was Dudley Stewart, I believe."

"That's what they're sayin'. We captured two of 'em, 'n they done been tried 'n found guilty, so we're fixin' to hang the sons of bitches soon as we can get the gallows built."

"I saw the construction down the street," Lucas said.

"Tell me, Mister, what can I get you?"

"A beer would be good."

The bartender drew the beer and set it on the bar, then picked up the half-dime Lucas had laid there.

"Did the sheriff go to the funeral, you suppose?"

"Well, purt nigh ever' one did, so I reckon he did, too. What you needin' the sheriff for?"

"I have some business to discuss with him," Lucas said, without being more specific.

"Well, I expec' he'll be back within the hour," the bartender said, a little miffed that his query wasn't more fully answered.

When Lucas finished his beer, he walked down to the sheriff's office. There was a deputy sitting there, with his feet propped upon the desk. Surprised by the visitor, the deputy swung his legs down.

"What do you want?" the deputy asked.

"I want to talk to Sheriff Hamby."

"The sheriff ain't here."

"That's all right, I can wait. May I speak with your prisoners?"

"You a lawyer? 'Cause iffen you are, it's too late. Them two's done been found guilty, 'n they're goin' to hang, come tomorrow."

"I'm not a lawyer."

"Newspaper man then?"

"No."

"Then what is it you're a' wantin' to see them two no accounts for then?"

"Like I said, I just want to talk to them."

"Well, I spec' you'd better wait 'n talk to the sheriff about that," the deputy said.

"That's all right. I'm quite ready to do that."

Lucas picked up a newspaper, then settled down to read.

When Sheriff Hamby returned about an hour later, he saw Lucas sitting quietly in a chair.

"Who's this? What's he doing here?" the sheriff asked his deputy.

"I don't know, he just said he wanted to talk to you," the deputy replied.

Hamby stepped over to his visitor. "Somethin' I can do for you, Mister?"

"Yes, you can let me talk to your prisoners."

"Why would you want to do that?"

"I'm hoping to get some information that will lead me to Dudley Stewart."

"Oh? Tell me, Mister, what do you want with Stewart?"

Dudley took out his badge to show Hamby.

"I'm a deputy US Marshal and I'm after Stewart."

"What's your name?"

"Lucas Cain."

Sheriff Hamby flashed a broad smile. "Lucas Cain? I'll be damn! Yes, you're the one who took out Bateman, aren't you?"

"Yes."

"Well, I want the son of a bitch caught, no matter who does it. And you have my blessing and any help I can give you."

"Thanks. The first thing I'll need is to talk to your prisoners."

"You can talk to 'em, but I don't know as you'll be able to get anything out of 'em."

"Let me try."

Sheriff Hamby made a motion toward the cell area in the back of the office. "Their names are Dobbins and Mathis. Have at it."

The two men were in the same cell, one of them was lying down on his bunk, the other, sitting on his.

"Which one of you is Dobbins?"

"Why do you need to know?" the one sitting on the bed answered. His shoulder was patched up. The other had a wrapped bandage around his upper leg.

"You're Dobbins I take it," Lucas said to the one who had spoken. "I would like to get some information about Dudley Stewart."

"We ain't goin' to tell you nothin'," Dobbins said.

"Really? You mean you're going to be loyal to Stewart after he left the two of you, so he could save his own skin?"

"Damn, he's right, Dan," Mathis said. "Why should we protect the son of a bitch after he run off like he done?"

11

The gallows was constructed in the middle of the street, and all who watched it go up, agreed that it was a work of art. Gruesome to be sure, but a work of art, never the less. Everyone in town was aware there was soon to be a hanging of course, and there was a morbid excitement as they awaited the upcoming event. When someone would point out that it wasn't right to be excited over something as gruesome as a hanging, they would be reminded of the seven citizens who were killed, including a little school girl and her teacher.

Friday morning, a sign was posted on the gallows to let everyone know who was about to be hanged, and why:

TO BE HANGED FROM THIS GALLOWS
AT HIGH NOON TODAY
DAN DOBBINS AND CARL MATHIS
FOR THE BRUTAL MURDER OF
SEVEN OF OUR CITIZENS

"I still don't know why you got to hang us," Dobbins said. "Hell, we didn't shoot that schoolmarm and the little girl. We was both lyin' on the ground, real bad shot up."

"You forget the five people who were killed during the hold up in the bank," Sheriff Hamby said.

"Yeah, but you ain't got no proof that me 'n Carl done that."

"It's like the judge said. It doesn't matter whether you're the ones who shot them or not. You were committing a felony by robbing the bank, and if anyone is killed during the commission of that felony, you're guilty of murder."

"That don't seem none right a' tall," Mathis said.

"Yeah, well you boys just stew on that for a while," Sheriff Hamby said. Leaving his two prisoners, he stepped back out to his desk.

A few minutes later, a tall, rather gaunt looking man wearing a black suit and a high hat came in.

"Sheriff, my name is Jason Claybaugh. I believe you have some business for me this morning."

"You're the hangman?"

"I am, sir."

"I wasn't sure you'd get here in time, but you've got two hours yet."

"I am always punctual, sir. Now, if I may, I would like to visit with the subjects."

"Subjects?"

"My customers, you might say. I always like to visit with them before I dispatch them to perdition."

"They're right back there. You'll find both in the same cell."

"That's very good of you to allow them to be together

like that. They are in their last moments, so it is good that they can give each other such comfort as is possible."

Claybaugh stepped back to the cells and saw the two men.

"Hello, gentlemen, allow me to introduce myself. My name is Jason Claybaugh, and at noon today, you and I will be the center of attention. And from all appearances, there will be a rather substantial crowd gathered to watch your departure from this earth.

"First, some preparations must be made, and for that I will need to know your weight. That way, I can make whatever adjustments as might be necessary, so that when you reach the bottom of your fall, you will die quickly with a broken neck, rather than hanging there gasping for breath, because if your neck doesn't break, you will be strangled.

"Mr. Mathis, if you would please, tell me how much you weigh."

"About a hunnert 'n eighty pounds, as far as I know," Mathis answered.

"And Mr. Dobbins?"

"I don't know. 'Bout a hunnert 'n sixty, I reckon."

"All right, thank you, that will do nicely. Now, one more thing. You have the option of having a hood put over your face before the drop is made. I strongly recommend that you choose to do so. It will not only protect you from the morbid stares of the crowd, it will also deny them the opportunity to see your face during your death throes."

"Yeah, I want the hood," Dobbins said.

"I don't want any hood. I want to stare at the sons of bitches before I go," Mathis said.

"Very well, gentlemen, you have been most helpful and I thank you. I must go now, there are a whole lot of people wanting me to autograph the souvenir program of the hanging. We will meet again at noon on the gallows platform. Until then, have a nice day."

As soon as Claybaugh left, another man came back to the cell to speak with them. Like Claybaugh, he was wearing a black suit, but rather than being tall and gaunt, he was short and plump, with a neck that rolled over his collar.

"Gentlemen, I am Reverend Galen Jessup, and I am here to offer you one last chance for the eternal salvation of your soul. Will you kneel now and ask God for His forgiveness?"

"Get outta here," Mathis said. "We don't need no preachin'."

"I wish I could change your minds, gentlemen, but we are each responsible for our own souls. I shall leave you to your own contemplations."

BY ELEVEN O'CLOCK A LITTLE more than three hundred people had gathered in town for the hanging. In addition to the town's people, many more were coming from the surrounding towns. They arrived on horseback, and in surreys, buckboards, and wagons. Because two of the murder victims had been from the school, school was let out for the day and benches were put on the very front row to accommodate those students who wished to come.

Vendors were working the crowd and one, Paul Dysert, who owned the photography studio, had set his camera up to he could take pictures of his paying customers, with the gallows in the background. Sweet cakes and coffee were being peddled, as well as beer.

About half-an-hour before the hanging was to take place, the Reverend Galen Jessup, of the Church of Redemption, climbed up onto the platform of the gallows, and began to take advantage of the opportune gathering cum congregation.

"Brothers and sisters, we are gathered here in the presence of God and in the shadow of this gallows, to send two unworthy sinners to their eternal punishment in the burning fires of hell. It need not have been this way. God forgives all sinners who come to Him for penance. I went to the two gentlemen you will see hanged here today, and I asked them to join me in a prayer of forgiveness but they denied the opportunity.

"Their souls are lost, but each of you has the opportunity to save your soul, by coming to church this Sunday, make an offering so that God's work may be continued, and ask His forgiveness for all your sins."

"Hey, preacher, this here ain't whiskey, it's communion wine," someone shouted, lifting a whiskey bottle to his lips.

A few in the crowd laughed nervously.

"Get off of there, preacher. We come here to see us a hangin', not listen to a preachin'," another from the crowd shouted, and while many laughed at the heckling, just as many were made uncomfortable by the taunt.

DOBBINS and Mathis could hear the sermon from their cell.

"Listen to that holy rollin' son of a bitch," Dobbins said with a derisive chuckle. "He's really preachin' hisself a sermon, ain't he?"

"You sound like you're enjoyin' it," Mathis said.

"Yeah, I am. It reminds me of bein' back in Arkansas. The whole family used to go out on an all-day preachin'. My old man would listen to it, get hisself some religion, then he'd come home and beat the hell out of ma and us kids because of the sinnin' he said we was doin'. Then, one day I decided I couldn't take it no more, so I picked up the shotgun 'n blowed his head off. I was fourteen." Dobbins laughed, insanely.

"I wish they would come for us, 'n get this over with," Mathis said.

LUCAS WAS STANDING with the others, when Sheriff Hamby and Deputy Barker brought the two condemned men from the jailhouse. Both prisoners had their hands handcuffed behind their back, and they kept their eyes straight ahead as they walked toward the gallows. Lucas had witnessed hangings before, often of men he had brought in. He didn't enjoy hangings, but he felt that it was his duty. In his opinion, it would be an act of cowardliness not to watch the results of his own actions.

Of course, he had nothing to do with the fate of these two men, but it was his intention to find, and bring to justice, Dudley Stewart. These two men had been part of Stewart's gang, and they had given him some information that might help him in his quest.

The hangman stood on the gallows platform exuding a sense of pride over the most prominent position he occupied in the drama that was about to be played out.

With Sheriff Hamby in front, and Deputy Barker behind, Mathis and Dobbins climbed the thirteen steps to the gallows platform. Sheriff Hamby positioned the two men, then Barker stepped back and Hamby turned to address the crowd.

"The two prisoners you see before you, Carl Mathis and Dan Dobbins, having been tried before a jury of their peers and found guilty, were sentenced to death by hanging, by Judge August P. Goodbody. As Sheriff of Santa Fe County, in the Territory of New Mexico, it is my duty to see that the judge's orders be carried out."

After delivering the order of execution, Hamby stepped over to the side of the platform, leaving the hangman, and the two condemned prisoners standing quietly. Claybaugh put the hood over the head of Dan Dobbins, then held the other hood out, offering Mathis one last opportunity to be blindfolded.

Mathis's response was the negative shake of his head.

The two men stood quietly as a noose was dropped around the neck of each of them. That done, Claybaugh walked over to the lever that would operate the trap door, then looked over toward the sheriff. After a barely perceptible nod of his head, Claybaugh pulled the lever back.

The trap doors over which Mathis and Dobbins were standing dropped open, and the two men fell through the opening. The ropes stopped them when they were about half-way through, then they twisted into a half turn, the ropes creaking in response.

Other than a collective gasp when the trap doors opened, there was a moment of stunned silence in the crowd.

While some remained in morbid curiosity, Lucas walked down to the saloon.

12

For the next two weeks after the hanging, Lucas tracked Stewart and his gang. The trail led to a cave, and rather than approach the cave on horseback, Lucas tied Charley II off where he could graze if he wanted to.

Pulling his pistol, Lucas advanced toward the cave by a circuitous route, moving from boulder to tree to ridgeline until he was just outside the opening. He paused for a long moment, listening.

He heard nothing. The silence may have been enough to send anyone else on their way without further investigation, but Lucas had a strong feeling that he should have a second look.

With gun in hand, Lucas approached the opening, staying to one side, rather than moving straight toward the mouth of the cave. He backed up to it for a closer listen.

He heard a woman crying.

He waited a few minutes longer to see if there was anyone who was talking. When he heard nothing, he eased his way into the cave and that was when he saw her. She was naked and bound head and foot to the wall. Her arms were tied down by her side so that she had no movement.

He searched as much of the cave as the ambient light would allow, but saw no one else. He approached the woman.

"No, please no!" the woman pleaded in a fear-laced voice. She drew her head back, which was basically the only movement left open to her.

Lucas holstered his pistol. "I'm not going to hurt you, Miss. I'm here to help you," he said. He drew his knife and started cutting away her bindings.

"Are you…are you one of them?" the woman asked.

"No, I'm not one of them. Who did this?" he asked.

"I don't know. There were several of them."

"Did one of them have a bulging eye?"

"Yes. You know them?"

"I know who they are. I'm looking for them," Lucas replied.

By now Lucas had cut all the restraints, and the woman stepped away from the wall of the cave.

"Do you, uh, have any clothes here?" Lucas asked.

"Oh! I'm naked!" the woman said, as if just realizing her condition.

"Do you have any clothes here?" Lucas repeated.

"I…I don't know. I was sleeping in my nightgown when they got me, but when I woke up, I was naked."

"I'll look around for you."

"Thank you."

Lucas looked around in the part of the cave that was illuminated by the light that came in through the mouth of the cave. Seeing nothing there, he gathered some straw, struck a match and made a torch to search back into the bowels of the mine. There, finding her nightgown in a pile, he brought it to her. The gown was badly torn, but it would, at least, restore some modesty.

"I won't look," he said, turning his back as she got dressed.

"That's all right," she said. "You've already seen me, and it isn't like I'm not seen by men just about every night."

"Oh, you're a—"

"Soiled dove is the genteel term," the woman said.

"That doesn't matter. You are still owed the courtesy of being able to dress in private."

"That's very nice of you."

"How did you wind up here?"

"One of the men wanted to take me upstairs, but he was drunk and he was mean, so I wouldn't go with him. The next morning, early, he and two more men came into my room and grabbed me. I tried to cry out but they held a handkerchief over my nose and mouth that smelled sort of sweet. The next thing I remember, I was tied up on a horse with someone behind me holding me on."

"Chloroform," Lucas said.

"What?"

"Chloroform. It's something doctors use to knock a person out when they're performing surgery. What's your name?"

"Jessie."

"Jessie what?"

"Just Jessie is enough. What is your name?"

"My name is Lucas. Where do you live, Jessie? I'll take you back home."

"Tesque. Do you know where that is?"

"I think I passed through it a month or so ago. It's ten or so miles north of here."

"Well, I know we were riding south when we left town. I don't know how far we came, and to be honest, I don't even know who it was who took me."

"They are outlaws led by Dudley Stewart. He's the one with the bad eye. They are a bunch of murdering, low-life, scum of the earth bastards. Excuse the language."

Jessie chuckled. "After what I've been through, a little bad language is nothing. You can turn around now. I'm as dressed as I can be under the circumstances, though I'm going to be quite a sight when we ride back into town."

"I have an idea. I've got another shirt, if you put it on, it might not look quite as much like a nightgown as your clothes do now."

"Thanks."

"It's pretty late now," Lucas said. "I would suggest that we spend the night here, so we can get a head start in the morning."

"No!" Jessie said, her voice constrained by quiet. "I'm afraid they'll come back."

"I want them to come back. They are the men I'm looking for."

"Please, no, don't make me stay here," Jessie pleaded.

Lucas cupped her chin and looked at the young woman. He could see the absolute fear in her eyes.

"All right, I'll take you on home."

It was dark when they rode into Tesque, riding double on Charley II. They passed by several houses which were just on the outside of the town. Most of the houses were softly lit by a single lantern or candles. As they rode on into the center of town, all the commercial business buildings were dark, but there were half-a-dozen buildings that were very brightly illuminated. The sounds of revelry spilled out into the street from each of them. Three of the buildings were identified as cantinas and three were saloons.

"That's where I live," Jessie said, pointing to one of the saloons. The name painted on the false front of the saloon read Fiddler's Green.

Lucas dismounted, tied Charley II to the hitching rail, then reached up to help Jessie down. He followed her into the saloon.

"Jessie!" someone shouted, then seeing Lucas behind her, added, "What the hell did you do to her, Mister?" He started toward Lucas with an angry expression on his face.

"No, George," Jessie said quickly. "This man saved my life!"

The expression on George's face changed from one of anger to appreciation.

"Well, in that case, Mister, I'd like to buy you a drink."

Lucas smiled. "And I'd like a beer, so that works out well."

"Step up to the bar," George said. "Abe, food, drink, anything he wants is on the house."

"Yes, sir, Mr. Steele," the bartender replied. "Beer, you said?" he asked, looking toward Lucas.

"Yes, thank you."

"Are you hurt?" one of the girls asked Jessie.

"They didn't beat me or anything. But it certainly wasn't pleasant."

"Come upstairs with me," the young woman invited. "Let's get you cleaned up."

A few of the men gathered around Lucas. They

wanted to know who he was, and how he happened to come across Jessie.

"I'm looking for Dudley Stewart and his gang," Lucas said. "I lost their trail, but then discovered a cave, and when I checked it out, I found Jessie. As it turns out, she had been taken to the cave by Stewart, but Stewart and the others had abandoned her there."

"Miller's Cave," George suggested.

"Miller's Cave?"

"It has to be. That's the only cave within a hundred miles, and I'm sure you didn't come a hundred miles today."

"I don't suppose any of you have any idea where I might find Stewart, do you?"

Lucas's question wasn't answered, so after a brief visit with those gathered around him, he took the saloon owner's offer of a meal.

Jessie came back downstairs to join Lucas for supper. She wasn't wearing the heavy makeup, nor the very revealing outfits as worn by the other girls; she was in fact, quite modestly dressed, and Lucas thought she was as beautiful as any young woman at a high-society social function.

"I'll ask you if you would like to come up to my room," Jessie said, over the meal.

"I appreciate the offer, but I feel I would be taking advantage of you," Lucas replied.

"You have to sleep somewhere, don't you?"

Lucas chuckled. "You have a point," he said.

LUCAS ROSE WITH THE SUN, the next morning. Getting dressed, he looked back at Jessie, who was still asleep.

Bending over, he kissed her on the cheek, but as he stood back up, Jessie smiled.

"Ummn, I like that," she said.

Lucas chuckled. "It was just a kiss on the cheek."

"Yes, but it was genuine," Jessie said, with a smile.

13

The sun was already low in the west when Lucas rode into the small town of Oje de la Vaca. The hollow clump of his horse's foot falls echoed back from the adobe buildings that surrounded the plaza. This town had a much stronger Mexican flavor than did Tesque, and the spicy aroma of Mexican cooking whetted his appetite.

Lucas rode up to the livery then dismounted.

"You want to leave your horse, *Señor*?" a boy of about fifteen asked.

Lucas dismounted, removed the saddlebags, and draped them across his shoulder, then pulled his rifle from the sheath.

"Yes. Can you give him a rub down and give him some oats?"

"*Si, Señor,* I can do this."

"Also, I'm looking for three men riding together. I think they may have come through here. They are outlaws, *bandidos*. Have you seen such men?"

"Maybe there were some men like that yesterday. I don't know."

"Did they leave their horses with you?"

"No, *Señor,* they left their horses tied in front of the cantina all night. When I looked for them this morning, they was gone."

"Can I get something to eat at the cantina?"

"*Si, Señor.* The tamales are very good, I think."

"*Muchas gracias,*" Lucas said.

"*No es nada,*" the young man replied with a smile.

Lucas walked across the plaza to the cantina. Unlike American saloons, such as Fiddler's Green, with the swinging batwing doors, the *Moneda de Plata Cantina* had several strings of brightly colored beads guarding the entrance. They made a clacking sound as Lucas pushed through them.

For a moment all conversation stopped as everyone looked toward him. The mix of customers was about equally divided between American and Mexican. The bartender was American, and he was busy lighting the lanterns on a wooden frame that was lowered from the ceiling.

"I'll be with you in a minute," he said.

The notice of the bartender triggered a response among the others so that a dozen or more conversations were renewed, Spanish and English in equal parts.

The pulley squeaked as the bartender pulled the frame back up, and the lanterns emitted a soft glow to illuminate the room.

"Now, what'll you have?"

"A beer and something to eat."

"What'll it be? We've got beans, beef, ham and eggs, or—"

"Tamales," Lucas said, interrupting the bartender.

The bartender smiled. "You must have boarded your horse with Miguel. His mama furnishes the tamales, and he touts them to everyone. The beef is better."

"Tamales," Lucas repeated.

"Have it your own way. Find a table, I'll bring 'em over to you."

Lucas found a table near the wall. Leaning his rifle against the wall, he dropped the saddlebags on the floor next to the table, then sat down. Almost immediately, a very pretty *señorita,* provocatively dressed, approached him.

"I will sit with you, *Señor,* if you will buy me a drink."

"Sure, why not?" Lucas replied.

"*Señor,* a drink please," she called over to the bartender. "My name is Maria," she said with a smile, as she joined Lucas at the table.

"Hello, Maria." Lucas didn't give his name.

"Have you come from far?"

Lucas chuckled. "Considering where I started from, I would say yes."

The bartender brought a drink for Maria, and a plate with two tamales for Lucas.

Lucas stripped the husks from the tamales, and took a bite. "Are you here every night, Maria?"

"Si, here is where I work."

"I'm looking for three men who may have been here last night. One has an eye that—"

Maria interrupted him before he could finish.

"*Un mal de ojo,* an evil eye," she translated. "*Si,* he was here."

"Where did they go?"

"*Señor,* the man with an evil eye. He is your friend?"

"No."

Maria reached across the table to put her hand on Lucas's hand.

"When a woman is…is with a man, she can tell many things about him. It is no accident that he has the mark of the devil. He is an evil man."

"You're right about that. Dudley Stewart is a long way from being a saint."

"If he is not your friend, why do you search for him?"

"He is wanted by the law."

"You are a lawman?"

"Yes."

"This is very dangerous, is it not?"

"Yeah, I suppose you could say that. Do you know where they went?"

"No. When I woke up this morning, my bed was empty. I heard them from outside, so I looked through my window."

"Which way did they go?"

"They went that way." Maria pointed in a southeast direction. She dropped her hand from his hand to his leg. "It is too late for you to look for them now, you will have to spend the night here. Would you like to stay with me tonight? I know I can please you very much."

Lucas reached down to take her hand, then move it from his knee to the table. He smiled at her.

"Maria, if I stayed with you tonight, I'm afraid I would want to spend every night with you, and if I did that, I would get no work done." He dropped a couple of coins on the table as he stood. "I'll be on my way, tomorrow, but thanks for the information."

"Lucas Cain," Maria called as Lucas started toward the door. "You must be very careful."

"I always try to be," Lucas replied.

It was dark now, and there were no streetlamps.

What little ambient light there was, did little to push away the darkness over the square. Lucas was a quarter of the way across the square before he stopped to think about Maria calling him by his full name. How did she know his name? He hadn't told her.

That bothered him enough that he decided he would go back and ask her, but just as he turned, two Mexicans came toward him from the shadows.

"Tonight, you will die, Lucas Cain," one of the men said. Both were brandishing knives, and they were making low, vicious swings. Lucas dropped his rifle into the dirt, and had it not been for his quick reflexes, the first swing would have disemboweled him.

Despite Lucas's quick move, one of the attackers did score, and Lucas felt a sharp pain in his side. Lucas fell, then rolled through the dirt to get away. He had no idea how bad the wound was, but it felt like someone was holding a hot poker against his side.

Seeing that Lucas was hurt, one of the attackers rushed forward to finish him off. As the attacker leaned over him, Lucas raised his legs and drove both his feet hard into the Mexican's groin, not only driving him back, but momentarily taking him out of the fight.

But the other man was still in it, and now he came toward Lucas. Lucas kicked him as well, but the second attacker managed to avoid it by jumping back. That did, however, give Lucas the opportunity to regain his feet. Once he was upright, he tried to draw his pistol, only to discover that it had fallen from his holster when he was down.

Realizing that Lucas was unarmed, his attacker approached him again, but before he could use his knife, Lucas thrust his fingers into the Mexican's eyes. The man screamed out in pain, dropped his knife, then fell to his knees with his hands over his eyes. Moving quickly, Lucas picked up the knife.

By now the first attacker had regained his feet, and he came charging toward him. Lucas twisted away to avoid the initial thrust, then counterthrust. His attacker, not realizing that Lucas was now armed, made no attempt to avoid Lucas's attack, and Lucas was able to bury the knife deep into the Mexican's chest. The blade was held sideways, so that it slipped in between the ribs, then Lucas turned it and let the Mexican tear himself off by his own weight. When the bloody knife was withdrawn, there was a large, jagged wound in the chest.

Lucas's would-be attacker's eyes opened wide in shock. He put his hand over his wound, and the blood spilled through his fingers. Then he dropped his knees, fell forward, and lay very still.

Quickly, Lucas recovered his rifle and pistol and turned toward the other man. He saw then that the second man offered no challenge. He was on his knees with his hands still covering his eyes. Lucas holstered his pistol.

By now, several had come out onto the square to see what was going on.

"Is there a sheriff in town?" Lucas asked.

"I'm the town marshal," one of the men said.

"I had no choice; they both came after me with knives."

"*Si*," Miguel, the stable boy said. "I saw what happened. It is true, what the *Americano* says."

"I believe you," the marshal said. "They are a bad lot. They probably saw you coming from the cantina, and thought you had some money on you. How about a couple of you men take this one down to the hardware store? Ellis can put his body in a sack, and we'll bury him tomorrow mornin'. I'll take this other one with me, and put him in jail. Get up, Jorge. Come with me."

"I am blind, *Señor* Perez. I cannot see," Jorge said.

"That's all right, I'll lead the way," Marshal Perez said.

"*Señor* Cain, you are hurt," Maria said. "Come to my room with me, and I will bandage you."

Until that moment, Lucas hadn't realized that Maria was there. Holding his hand over his side, he followed her into the cantina, then up the stairs. A couple of times as he was climbing the stairs, he had to stop and lean against the wall. Each time he did so, he left his mark, in a smear of blood.

When they reached the top of the stairs, Maria opened the door, then lit a lantern. "Sit here," she said, pointing to the bed.

Lucas followed her instructions, then winced as she removed his shirt. The side where he was wounded was covered with blood. Pouring water from a large, earthen jug, into a pan, she began, gently, to wash away the blood. Then she opened the drawer to a chifforobe and removed a petticoat from which she tore strips to make a bandage.

"Did you know those two men?" Lucas asked.

"*Si*. The one you killed was Lopez. The one you made blind was Jorge. They were both evil men, and I think they meant to steal money from you."

"No, they weren't after my money, and you know it."

Maria gasped. "Why do you say such a thing?"

"You set me up."

"*Señor,* I do not know what this means, to set you up."

"You may not know the words, but you sure know how to do it. How did you know my name, Maria?"

"*Qué?*"

"As I was leaving the cantina, you called me by first and last name. How did you know my name?"

Maria didn't answer. Instead, she continued in silence, to work on the bandage. Lucas reached down and squeezed her wrist.

"*Señor,* you are hurting me," Maria said, wincing in pain. Tears came to her eyes.

"How did you know my name?" Lucas repeated.

"The man you are looking for, the man with the evil eye, paid Lopez and Jorge to kill you. Then, Lopez and Jorge described you to me, and said you would come soon."

"And you, Maria, how much did they pay you? Did they pay you thirty pieces of silver?"

"No, *Señor,* do not say that I am as one who betrayed Jesus." Maria crossed herself. "They paid me nothing. *Nada.*"

"If they paid you nothing, then why did you do it?"

Maria walked to a corner that was blocked off by a screen. She stepped behind it for a moment, then reappeared, holding a baby. She held the baby to her face, as her eyes filled with tears.

"They told me if I did not do this for them, they would kill my baby. I am sorry, *Señor*. Please *perdóname*. Forgive me. I could not let anything happen to my baby."

Lucas sighed and reached for his shirt. "All right," he said, as he put the shirt on over his bandage. "I understand."

"Where will you go now?"

"I am going after Stewart and his men."

"But you are hurt. Stay here, with me."

"Thanks, but I think it would be better if I stayed in the hotel tonight. Thanks for patching me up."

"*Señor* Cain?" Maria called as Lucas started toward

the door. He stopped and turned toward her. She continued. "You must be very careful. When the man you are after learns that Jorge and Lopez did not kill you, they will hire others."

"I'm sure they will."

"But it will be very dangerous for you. How will you know who is your enemy and who is your friend?"

Lucas flashed a sardonic smile. "That's easy, darlin'. I have no friends."

14

Within a few weeks after Dobbins and Mathis were hanged back in Dos Nachos, Stewart had brought in two more men, Herman Owens, and Pete Bundy to replace them. Now Stewart, Calhoun, and the two new men were waiting just outside of Oje de la Vaca as the night creatures serenaded each other. They could hear the strum of a guitar from the cantina, and the sound of a piano from the saloon. It had been over an hour since Stewart had sent Coker in to find out what had happened.

"Where the hell is he?" Calhoun asked. "Coker should be back by now to tell us what happened."

"I'll tell you what happened," Bundy said. "Ole' Cain is a' lyin' in the street gutted and dead by now. 'N what Coker is doin' is havin' hisself a drink in the cantina to celebrate."

"I wouldn't be all that sure about that," Calhoun said.

"Why do you say you ain't sure?" Bundy asked. "I know them two men and they're very good at what they do. 'N what with Cain not even a' lookin' out for 'em, they prob'ly had him gutted like a hog a'fore he even know'd they was there."

"You don't know Cain. He's always on the watch."

"Yeah, but he's just one man. 'N Lopez 'n Jorge are damn good with knives."

"Hush up, both of you," Stewart hissed. "Someone's comin'."

"Coker, you think?" Calhoun asked.

"Maybe, but let's be ready just in case," Stewart said.

Stewart and the others drew their guns, then got behind the rocks to wait for whoever was coming.

"It's Coker," Calhoun said, after a moment or two.

"It's about damn time," Bundy said.

The men holstered their pistols, then stepped out to welcome Coker's return.

Coker dismounted, then tossed a bottle of whiskey to Calhoun. "Thought you boys might like this."

"Yeah, thanks," Calhoun said, smiling as he pulled the cork, then turned the bottle up for a drink. Then, lowering the bottle, he ran the back of his hand across his lips, before passing the bottle on to Bundy.

"Well?" Stewart asked, his deformed eye fixing as steady a gaze toward Coker as the other.

"Any coffee left?" Coker asked. He walked over to the campfire, found a tin cup, then poured coffee from the pot that was sitting on a nearby rock. He took a swallow, then let out a sigh of contentment. "They ain't nothin' that's no better than coffee when you're still up, late in the night."

"Damn it, Coker, what the hell happened?" Stewart demanded.

"Nothin' happened," Coker said as he took another drink of the coffee.

"Nothing?"

"Well, nothin' that's good for us, that is. That Cain, what he done was, he kilt Lopez, 'n he blinded Jorge. Let me tell you somethin' in case you ain't figured it out yet, that sumbitch'n Cain takes a heap o' killin'."

"Damn," Stewart said, striking his open palm with his fist. "I should 'a knowed better 'n to hire a couple of Mexicans to do the job. I paid 'em twenty dollars apiece to kill Cain. Now I'm out forty dollars, 'n Cain is still alive."

"Well, Dudley, it ain't like they didn't try," Calhoun said. "It's like Coker just told us, one of 'em is blind, 'n the other'n is kilt."

"Yeah? Well, good enough for 'em, 'far as I'm concerned, they didn't try hard enough," Stewart said.

"What are we goin' to do now?" Coker asked. "Him still bein' alive, means he's goin' to be comin' after us. We can't just wait around here, can we?"

"I don't know, I don't know," Stewart said. "Just give me time, I'll think of somethin'."

"Maybe you won't have to think of nothin'," Coker said. He took another swallow of coffee, then continued, with amazing calmness. "It could be that it's goin' to be took care of for us."

"What do you mean?" Stewart asked.

"Do you know Jeb Boyle?"

"No, I ain't never heard of 'im. Why do you ask?"

"Jeb Boyle, 'n two of Boyle's cousins come down here from Colorado. They was all talkin' in the saloon, 'n I was listenin' in without them a' knowin' that I was listenin'. They been doggin' Cain's tail, all the while he's been doggin' your'n."

"Why are they after Cain?" Stewart asked.

"It turns out that back in Colorado, Cain kilt Ely Boyle, him bein' Jeb Boyle's brother. They've found out that Cain is in town, 'n they're plannin' on killin' him, first thing in the mornin'. So it could be that Cain's goin' to be took care of for us, 'n it won't cost you another forty dollars."

Stewart smiled. "Well, all right then, this might just work out real good for us."

JEB BOYLE and his two cousins, Lyman and Kurt Boyle were waiting in the livery just as the sun came up the next morning. Miguel, the young stable boy, was sitting in the corner, bound and gagged.

"You sure he's comin' here?" Lyman asked.

"You heard, same as I did, that he was plannin' on leavin' town today," Jeb said. "He won't be walkin', when he leaves, 'n that means he'll be comin' here to get his horse. 'N when he comes, we'll kill 'im."

"It's too bad them two Mexicans didn't kill 'im when they jumped 'im last night," Lyman said.

"No, I'm just as glad they didn't kill 'im. I want the pleasure of killin' 'im myself," Jeb said.

"You ain't plannin' on callin' 'im out are you?" Kurt asked. "On account of if you do, I don't want nothin' to do with it. You know how good that sumbitch is at drawin', 'n shootin'."

"I don't plan on callin' 'im out, all I want to do is kill 'im. There's three of us, 'n one of him. I figure we can shoot 'im as soon as he comes into the livery, 'n he won't even know we're here."

"Yeah," Lyman said. "That's the best way to do it."

"What about him?" Kurt asked, pointing to Miguel.

"He's heard us talkin', so he knows who we are. We'll kill 'im, too, soon as we got Cain kilt."

LUCAS HAD a breakfast of ham and eggs, and he was enjoying a second cup of coffee. His side was still sore, but it wasn't bothering him as much now as it did last night. Also, he was glad to see that no blood had seeped through on the bandage Maria had applied last night. He wasn't all that surprised by the absence of blood, he learned last night that the cut, though painful, was not very deep.

Finishing his coffee, Lucas retrieved his rifle, which was leaning against the wall of the café, paid a quarter for his breakfast, then started toward the livery to get his horse. As he approached the stable, he saw a bird start to fly in through the open door, but quickly turn and fly away. The average person would not take any notice of the bird's action, but, because Lucas Cain was a man who lived his life on the edge, he was always attuned to the slightest nuance, and he realized there must be some reason why the bird didn't go into the building.

Because of that, Lucas didn't go into the livery barn. Instead, he showed no reaction at all, and he walked on by without even a glance toward the door.

"WHAT THE HELL?" Lyman asked. "Why didn't he come in?"

"He must 'a seen us," Kurt said.

"No, that's impossible," Jeb said. "We're too far back in the shadows. He must be goin' to have his breakfast before he leaves. It won't be long now, so we'll just wait on 'im."

"Why don't we look out 'n see where he's goin'?" Lyman suggested.

"No, he might see us." Jeb said. "The way it is now, he don't have no idea that we're in here. Just be patient, he'll come in here soon. I've waited long enough so I can wait a little longer."

THE LAST BUILDING on this side of the street was White's Apothecary. As soon as Lucas passed it, he turned to go around it, then came out in the alley behind. He followed the alley past the apothecary, the barber shop, Travers's Grocery Store, the Lady's Millinery, Saddle and Leather goods, the blacksmith shop, then found himself behind the livery.

A rope was hanging down from the hayloft, and leaning his rifle against the back wall, he used the rope to climb up into loft. The first thing he did after reaching the loft, was to put his hand on the bandage, to make certain no blood had seeped through, and was pleased to find that it had not.

Lucas drew his pistol, then walked quietly across the loft so that he could look below. He wasn't surprised to see three men standing just behind the door, with guns drawn.

"You men wouldn't be looking for me, would you?" he called down to them.

"Damn, it's Cain, in the loft! How the hell did he get up there?" Jeb shouted, and jerking his pistol around he fired a shot.

The bullet from Jeb's gun didn't even come close, but Lucas returned fire, and a pink mist of blood sprayed from the hole in Jeb's forehead.

Lyman fired at Lucas, but so quickly had Lucas reacted from shooting at the first man, that his bullet hit Lyman in the shoulder of his gun hand, and the result caused him to drop his gun before he could even take aim. As a result, his bullet, too, went wide.

Because he was Lucas's third target, Kurt was able to get his shot off, unaffected by Lucas. Kurt's bullet slammed into the rafter overhead. Lucas's return shot hit Kurt in the knee, and with a sharp call of pain, he put his hand over his knee and collapsed. Now two men were down, and the third was holding his hand over the wound in his shoulder.

"Who the hell are you? And why did you try to kill me?"

Lyman pointed to the man who was now lying very still on the floor of the barn. "That there is Jeb Boyle. You kilt his brother, Ely. I'm Lyman Boyle, 'n the one you shot in the knee is Kurt. We're Jeb 'n Ely's cousins, so Jeb come to us to help 'im get even with you."

"You still planning on tryin' to get even with me?" Lucas asked.

Lyman pointed to Jeb's body. "Mister, far as I'm concerned, them two brothers is eatin' breakfast together in hell right now. I don't want nothin' more to do with it, 'n I don't reckon my brother does neither."

Lucas climbed down from the loft, then saw, for the first time that Miguel was tied and gagged. He walked over to untie him, just as the marshal came into the livery with his own gun drawn.

"You again," Perez said, the tone of his voice indicating no surprise.

"This was not *Señor* Cain's doing," Miguel said. "Those three men were waiting to kill him. They tied me up so I could not call out to *Señor* Cain and warn him."

"Cain, you better look out," Perez said. "Seems to me like you might just run out of bullets, before you run out of enemy."

"Could be," Lucas answered laconically. "Could be."

"Come on, you two," Jessup said to Lyman and Kurt. "You two are goin' to jail."

"We need doctorin'," Lyman said.

"Only kind of doctor we got is a horse doctor, but I'll get him down to see you, soon as I get you both in jail." Perez turned to look at Lucas. "Cain, I hope you're plannin' on leavin' town pretty soon. You seem to be keepin' our undertaker busy, 'n our jail full."

Lucas threw his saddle over Charley II, and tightened the cinches. "Is now soon enough for you?" he asked as he swung into the saddle.

Perez smiled. "Yeah, I'd say now is a good time."

15

It was now two weeks, and as many towns since Lucas had left Oje de la Vaca. It was late afternoon, and the sun was a brilliant red orb, one disk above the western horizon, when Lucas saw the little mining town of San Domingo. A shimmer of red sunlight bounced off the few dozen buildings that were clustered on the side of the mountain before him. This was a mining community, as evidenced by the zig-zagging wooden trestles that were higher up on the mountain behind the town.

Lucas's horse, noticing that they were approaching a town, quickened his pace, figuring that he would get rest and food there. As Lucas rode into town, he saw a sign advertising the Gold Nugget Cantina, and thinking that a beer and something to eat would be good, he decided to check it out as soon as he had Charley II taken care of.

When he stopped at the livery stable, he gave the hostler two dollars extra to get oats and a rub down for his horse. Leaving the stable, he walked across the street then down the boardwalk passing a number of buildings on the way to the saloon. The painting of a mug of beer, gold with a white foam head, was so realistic looking, he could almost taste it. He pushed through the doors and stepped inside.

There were about a dozen men, and one woman in the saloon. Three of the men were standing at the bar, the others scattered among the tables. The woman, who was Mexican, was sitting in a chair at the back wall where a piano would have been if the saloon had had a piano.

There were three very muscular looking men sitting at one of the tables, and because of the way they were dressed, Lucas figured them to be miners rather than cowboys. The woman, seeing a new man come into the saloon, approached him with a practiced smile. Lucas guessed she was in her mid-thirties, though her eyes looked much older.

"Buy me a drink, *Señor*?"

"Sure, why not?" Lucas said, returning her smile.

"My name's Sofia."

"Good to meet you, Sofia. I'm Lucas."

"Have you come to work in the mines, or are you prospecting?"

"I guess you could say I'm prospecting. I'm looking for some men, but I don't know their names."

Sofia laughed. "How can you look for men if you don't know their names?"

"I do know the name one of them. His name is Dudley Stewart. He's the leader of the group, and he's as ugly as a turnip. He has a bad eye, looks like it's 'bout to pop out of its socket."

Sofia chuckled. "I have seen many men who are as ugly as a turnip, but I do not think I have seen someone with an eye like that. But if I do see him, shall I tell him you are looking for him?"

"Ha!" Lucas replied. "There's no need for you to do that. This fella not only knows that I'm looking for him, he's doing everything he can to keep me from finding him."

"Why do you look for him? Are you a lawman, or a bounty hunter?"

"Does it make any difference?" Lucas asked.

"No, *cariño*, not to me, it doesn't."

Lucas turned toward the others in the saloon and asked in a voice loud enough to be heard by all.

"I'm looking for Dudley Stewart, or any man who rides with him. Do any of you know him, or have you seen him? If so, I'd be much obliged for your answer."

The three big men that Lucas had taken for miners, nodded at each other, then got up to leave.

"What about you men?" Lucas asked. "Do you know Stewart, or any of his men?"

"No," one of them said, the answer short and gruff.

Lucas watched them walk out of the saloon.

"I sort of get the idea that those men wouldn't like to have a friendly drink with me," Lucas said.

"Don't think anything about that. They aren't friendly with anyone. But I, on the other hand," she paused in mid-sentence, "can be very friendly." She let the last four words slide out in a throaty, seductive tone. "I've got a room upstairs where I can show you just how friendly I can be. If you're interested, that is."

"Not now," Lucas said. "Truth is, darlin', I've just got too much on my mind now. Maybe later."

"All right," she said. "I'll be here anytime you want me."

IT WAS JUST AFTER SUPPER, and Lucas walked over to the livery barn to check on Charley II, when he saw the three men who he had taken as miners, step out into the alley between the stalls. One of them went back to the barn door, and locked it shut.

"Well, hello, again," Lucas said. "You wouldn't talk to me in the saloon. You ready to talk to me now, are you?"

"Ha, what do you think, Lenny? He wants to talk to us," one of the men said.

"I ain't changed my mind, Clem. What about you, Moe?" Lenny asked the man who had closed and locked the door. "You changed your mind?"

"Nah, I ain't changed my mind," Moe answered.

"I've sort of got the idea that this isn't going to be a very friendly meeting, is it?" Lucas asked. His voice was as calm as if he had just ordered a beer.

The calmness of his voice startled the three men, who had expected him to show fear.

Though night had fallen, the stable was illuminated by the soft glow of a few lanterns that hung from the stanchions.

"If you aren't going to talk, what do we do now?" Lucas asked.

"First thing you can do is shuck that pistol belt," Clem said.

"Why would I want to do that?"

"On account of if you don't do it, I'm goin' to open up your spine with this here double-barrel twelve-gauge shotgun," Moe said.

Lucas felt the shotgun being jammed into his back.

"If you're going to shoot me with that shotgun, there's no need for me to drop my gun and holster, is there? So just go ahead and do it."

Lenny smiled, causing his teeth to gleam yellow in

the flickering light. Lenny was the only one who had a beard.

"You know what, Mister? You got guts. I like you. I wouldn't want anything to do with someone who don't have guts."

"Only, we ain't being paid to kill you. We're just being paid to beat you up," Moe added.

"And we ain't goin' to do nothin' we ain't gettin' paid to do," Clem added.

"Beat me up? That's strange, I can't see Dudley Stewart paying someone to beat me up. Kill me, maybe, but not beat me up."

"Well, there you go then," Lenny said. "Dudley Stewart don't have nothin' to do with this here ass-whuppin' we're a' gonna give you."

"I'm curious then. Who is paying you to do this?"

"It's a feller named Bryan Mooney. He give us ten dollars apiece to take you down a peg or two. He says it's for what you done to him back in Ortiz."

Lucas unbuckled his holster and let it drop. "Yeah, I guess I did knock him around a bit." Lucas chuckled. "So he's hired you three to get even for him, has he?"

"Mister, I don't know what the hell you can find to laugh about," Lenny said. "We're about to beat the hell out of you."

"Well, in that case, you don't mind if I start first, do you?" Lucas asked, and catching the three miners off-guard, he hit Lenny in the nose with a short, but powerful punch.

"Oh, you son of a bitch!" Lenny shouted. Blood spewed from his nose, across his mouth, getting on his teeth and down onto his chin.

From behind him, Moe slammed the butt of the shotgun hard between his shoulder blades. Lucas felt an explosion of pain throughout his whole body. His knees buckled, and he lurched forward a couple of stutter steps.

Moe, taking advantage of Lucas's temporary condition, sent a club-like blow on the side of his head, just above the ear, and by now, Lenny had recovered enough to catch Lucas with a solid blow to the point of his chin. Lucas saw stars.

The three miners relaxed a little. Each one of them was sure he would be a match for Lucas in a one-on-one fight. With the three of them, there was no fight. They were just performing a task, such as excavating so many tons of rock from the mine where they worked.

"You two stand back and let me have the son of a bitch," Lenny said, the blood running across his lips bubbling as he spoke. "I owe 'im."

The other two men stood back to give Lenny the opportunity to end it on his own. But before Lenny could throw a punch, Lucas held his palm flat, then struck Lenny in the solar plexus with a strong jab of the ends of his fingers, which had the effect of knocking the breath out of his adversary.

Lenny let out a whoosh as his face turned blue, and clasping both hands over his belly, he leaned forward.

Lucas took advantage of Lenny's condition to throw a roundhouse blow to his jaw, knocking him down. Lenny made no effort to regain his feet.

With an angry shout, Clem and Moe closed in on Lucas, and though he tried to fend them off, he was pummeled by the sledgehammer like blows to his head and body from the two muscular men. Even when he was able to raise his arms to deflect the blows, the result was a numbing of his arm.

He realized that it was useless to try and ward off the

pounding from the two miners, so he decided to try and get as many punches in as he could. He scored one against Moe's eye and another against Clem's jaw, but that didn't even slow them down. Blow after blow rained down on Lucas until he drew himself up into as tight a ball as he could as they continued to pummel him. Finally, he was no longer able to maintain his feet, so he fell to the ground.

Clem and Moe began kicking him.

"That's enough, that's enough!" Lenny called. "We were paid to beat 'im up, not kill 'im, 'n I ain't doin' nothin' no more 'n we're gettin' paid to do."

"What are we goin' to do with him?" Moe asked.

"We'll just leave 'im here," Lenny said.

"What about Mooney?" Clem asked.

"What about 'im?" Lenny asked.

"Shouldn't we tell 'im what we done?"

"Why? He's done paid us, 'n I'm through with 'im."

Lenny looked down at Lucas.

"I'll tell you this, Lucas Cain. You're one hell of a man," he said, begrudgingly. "Come on, let's go," he said to the others.

The three miners left Lucas lying in the dirt between the rows of stalls. Lucas waited until the three were gone before he tried to get up. He discovered that he wasn't able to stand, and when he put his hand over his side, he came away with blood. The wound on his side had been reopened. Exhausted, he lay there breathing heavily.

From the cantina across the street, he heard the high-pitched trill of a woman's happy scream, followed by the loud guffaw of a man's laugh. In the street in front of the livery, he heard the clopping sound of a horse and rider passing by. Everywhere else, life was going on as normal, while inside, Lucas was fighting just to stay conscious.

Painfully, laboriously, Lucas managed to get onto his hands and knees, and he crawled over the nearest stall. There, he used the boards to pull himself up onto his feet. Once he was up, though, he felt totally exhausted from the effort, so he had to lean against the stall for several moments while he recovered enough strength to stand on his own.

Lucas began to examine his body to determine if any bones had been broken. He checked his ribs, collarbone, legs, arms, and fingers. He decided that nothing had been broken, but the wound had been reopened, and though it wasn't bleeding profusely, it was bleeding. And, he had to admit, this was the worst beating he had ever taken.

He heard someone come into the livery, and he reached for his gun, only to remember that it was lying in the dirt where he had left it. If someone was coming in to kill him now, it would be little more than an execution. Maybe that's what Mooney wanted, to have the miners make him incapable of defending himself so he could be easily killed. Well, they would have to find him first. Lucas moved into the shadows of the empty stall where he was standing.

"*Señor* Lucas? *Señor* Lucas, are you in here?"

It was Sofia.

"*Señor* Lucas?"

Was this another setup? Or was she genuinely concerned for him? He decided to take a chance.

"I'm here, Sofia," he called quietly. "In this stall."

He staggered out of the stall, and Sofia hurried to him.

"*Dios mío*," she gasped when she saw him. "They nearly killed you."

"How did you know I was in here?" Lucas asked, suspiciously.

"The three men who did this came back to the cantina and they were bragging about what they had done. But, from the looks of things, they were telling the truth."

"How did they look?"

Sofia couldn't help but laugh at the question. "They did not look good, *Señor* Lucas. Not nearly as bad as you, but not good."

Lucas chuckled. "Good. They may have gotten a meal, but I got a sandwich."

"Why did they do this?" Sofia asked.

"It was nothing personal. They were just delivering a message from a friend."

"Oh? Some friend," Sofia said with an arched eyebrow.

16

Lucas had no idea why there was a drum beating in his head. He also had no idea where he was, or how he had gotten there. He lay there, wherever 'there' was for a long moment, before he opened his eyes. He was in bed, in a room that was brightly lit by sun rays spilling in through the window. The drumming in his head subsided, and he could smell perfume. There was a familiarity to the scent, and he recognized it as the perfume Sofia had been wearing.

Was this her room?

He looked around the room for her, but didn't see her.

"Sofia?" he called, remembering at that moment that she had helped him walk over from the livery last night. Or at least he assumed it was last night.

"Sofia?" he called again.

There was no answer to his call.

The drumming in his head began anew, and this time it was louder and even more intrusive than it had been earlier. It took but a moment for Lucas to realize that the drumming he was hearing was actually someone pounding, very loudly, on the door.

"Yeah, keep your pants on, I'm coming," Lucas said as he swung his feet over the edge of the bed. His pistol lay on the table beside the bed, and he picked it up, then started toward the door, feeling pain in every part of his body.

Holding the pistol at the ready, he jerked the door open. A tall man, with clear blue eyes and a sweeping moustache, stood just on the other side of the door. He was wearing a star pinned to his vest.

"You're Lucas Cain?" the visitor asked.

"Who wants to know?"

"My name's Vernon Cox. I'm the city marshal here, and I could use your help."

"My help?"

"Yeah. A couple of men just took over the Ace High Saloon, 'n they've run ever' body out. When I went down there to talk to 'em, they ran me off, and told me they would kill me if I came back."

Lucas stepped back from the door by way of inviting the marshal in. Then he walked over to the chifforobe, poured a pitcher of water into a pan, washed his face, then reached for a towel before he responded to Cox's request.

"Well, you're a city marshal, seems to me like threats like that come with the territory," Lucas said.

"I ain't denyin' that, Marshal," Cox replied, "but that don't mean I can't ask for help, does it? Especially if it concerns you."

"What do you mean, if it concerns me?"

"The bartender said they was there, lookin' for you."

"Did he, now? Who are they?"

"One of 'em's called Taylor, 'n the other one is Crowley. Ever heard of 'em?"

"No, I don't think so."

"Yeah, well, they've sure heard of you. You're the reason they come here in the first place."

"So the bartender says."

"What do you say, Marshal? Will you help me? This should be right down your alley. I've heard that you're a U.S. Marshal, but that the only pay you get is whatever bounty there is. There's paper out on both of these guys. Are you sure you haven't heard of 'em?"

"I'm not sure whether I have or not. I think I may have seen something on them, but they can't be worth much, or I would, for sure, know about them. I doubt they're worth going after."

"Maybe they're not worth chasing all over the country after, but you don't have to go anywhere to look for 'em. They're right here, 'n since I can't collect any of the reward money it would go to you. All I'm askin' is, that you just give me a hand bringin' 'em in."

"All right," Lucas agreed. He pulled on his pants, then reached for his boots. "Just give me a couple of minutes to get dressed, and I'll go down there with you."

"I appreciate it," Cox said. "Truth is, I'm gettin' a little old for this sort of thing. 'Bout all I'm good for these days is breakin' up fights, 'n runnin' in drunks."

"Breaking up fights, you say? I was in a fight last night. Where were you when I needed you?"

"I'm sorry 'bout that, Cain. Truth is, I didn't hear nothin' 'bout it 'til the fight was already over. But if you want me to, I'll run them three boys into jail now, for what they done to you last night."

"No, leave 'em alone. There's no real harm done. I

mean they could've quite easily killed me if they had wanted to, but they didn't."

What Lucas didn't say was that he wasn't sure Cox could run them in, even if he had tried.

Lucas reached for his hat. "Let's go."

As Lucas and Marshal Cox walked down toward the Ace High Saloon, he saw that word of the impending showdown had spread through town. Men, and some women as well, were already gathered in little groups, in the street and on the boardwalks, looking toward the Ace High Saloon in anticipation of what was about to happen.

Among those gathered, were the three men he had encountered last night. They were standing in front of the hardware store.

Lenny had his nose bandaged, and Clem and Moe were both sporting black eyes. Lucas smiled at them, then nodded his head in recognition. To his surprise, all three of the men returned his greeting with rather wan smiles.

A shot rang out from the saloon, and a bullet hit the dirt right in front of Lucas and Cox.

"That's far enough," someone called from the saloon.

"Taylor, Crowley, I want you two men to put your guns down, and your hands up. Then I want you to come walkin' out here toward us.

"We don't plan on doin' nothin' like that," one of the two men replied. "If you want us, you're goin' to have to come in here 'n get us."

"I'm ready to do that," Cox replied. "But I think you should know that this fella with me is U.S. Marshal Lucas Cain. And if I have to come after you, Cain will be comin' with me."

"Wait, wait!" a voice called from inside. "There ain't

no need for nothin' like that. Cox, why don't you just come in alone, so's we can talk things over?"

"Don't do it, Marshal," Lucas said. "You don't have anything to gain by doing that. Just tell them to come out."

Marshal Cox looked toward the saloon as if studying it for a moment. "I don't know, Cain. Seems to me like my job as city marshal ought to be to settle this thing without 'ny shootin' if I can. I can't see as it would hurt anything for me to just go inside 'n see what they have to say."

Lucas shook his head. "I wouldn't go in there if I were you, Cox. I don't have a good feeling about this."

"Yeah, well, like I said, it's my duty to take care o' this the best way I can. So even if I had the same feelin' you do, I'd still have to do ever' thin' I can to end it peaceable."

"I'm telling you, I know that there's no need for you to take any unnecessary chances. I wish you would listen to me. But if you for sure are going in there, I'm going with you."

Cox took his pistol belt and hung it across the nearby hitching rail. "No, they said come alone, 'n that's what I intend to do. Promise me you won't do anything to rile 'em up while I'm in there."

"I won't," Lucas promised.

Marshal Cox put his hands up, then started toward the saloon. "All right, fellas, I'm unarmed, 'n I'm comin' in now."

Lucas followed Cox to the front of the saloon, then he stepped into the alley and drew his gun and waited as Cox, with his hands still up, pushed in through the swinging batwing door.

Cox had no sooner stepped inside, before Lucas heard a shot being fired.

Almost immediately thereafter, Cox came staggering back outside, holding his hands over his chest. Blood oozed between his fingers.

"I should 'a listened to you," Cox said in a strained voice. "I've been kilt."

Cox fell face down into the street in front of the saloon, and several of the townspeople let out gasps of surprise and anger.

Lucas hurried over to the marshal, and as he knelt to check on him, he heard the crashing of glass as a chair was thrown through the front window. One of the two men, Lucas didn't know if it was Taylor or Crowley, leapt through the opening thus made.

"That's Taylor! He's gettin' away!" one of townspeople shouted.

As soon as Taylor jumped outside, he turned his gun toward Lucas and pulled the trigger. Lucas felt the concussion of the bullet as it whizzed by his head, and he returned fire. The bullet energized by Lucas's gun plowed into Taylor's knee, and Lucas saw blood and pieces of bone exit the wound. Taylor cried out in pain and went down.

By now the other man had entered the fray, jumping through the broken window. He ran for cover behind the watering trough that was in front of the bootmaker's shop. The townspeople who had gathered to watch the events unfold, hurried out of the way, emitting shouts of fear as they did so. Whereas a moment earlier they had been spectators, now they were running for their lives.

Lucas, realizing that he was exposed, lay down behind the porch. The porch was low, so that the only way Lucas could gain any cover, was to lie as close to the ground as he could.

"Taylor! Taylor, why ain't you shootin'?" Crowley called from behind the watering trough.

"I'm shot bad," Taylor replied, his agonized cry laced with pain.

"Where you hit?"

"In the leg."

"In the leg? Hell, that ought not to keep you from shootin'. Shoot 'im! Shoot the son of a bitch!" Crowley shouted.

Crowley followed his shout with a shot, and Taylor shot as well. Taylor's effort came closest, the bullet skidding across the floor of the porch, and Lucas could feel his face stinging with a spray of splinters.

"You're out in the open, Taylor," Lucas called. "Throw your gun away and lie still or I'll shoot you again, and this time it won't be in your leg."

"All right, don't shoot, don't shoot!" Taylor pleaded. "Look, I'm throwing it away!" Taylor tossed the gun out into the middle of the street.

"Taylor, you cowardly son of a bitch!" Crowley shouted, following his harsh words with gunshot.

Taylor put his hands over the wound in his belly, and fell.

When Crowley shot Taylor, Lucas took advantage of Crowley's exposure. Lucas pulled the trigger, and Crowley went down. Giving up his cover behind the porch, Lucas walked over to examine the two men. Taylor was lying on his back—Crowley was face down in the dirt, with a pool of blood spreading under his head.

Taylor was gasping for breath.

Lucas left Taylor, who was fighting for every breath he took, then hurried over to check on the marshal. Cox lay on his back. His eyes were open and at first glance, Lucas thought he might still be alive. As he looked more closely though, he realized that the eyes, though open, were devoid of any life.

"How's the marshal?" someone called.

"He's dead, I'm afraid," Lucas said.

"What about them other two?"

"Crowley's dead, Taylor is still alive," one of the townspeople called back.

"Then by damn, if the son of a bitch is still alive, somebody get a rope!" another said.

"You won't need a rope," Lucas said. "He'll be dead before you can string him up."

Taylor coughed, and blood came from his mouth.

"Did you kill Crowley?" Taylor asked.

"Yeah, I killed him."

"Good, I'm glad the son of a bitch is dead."

"You killed the marshal if that's what you two set out to do," Lucas said. "But it cost both of you your lives."

"We wasn't after Cox," Taylor said, wheezing out the words. "We was after you."

"Yes, so the marshal said."

"We thought we could get you before you even know'd we was after you." Taylor had a fit of coughing, and more blood poured from his mouth.

"Five hunnert dollars," he said.

"What do you mean, five hundred dollars?"

"That's how much Dudley Stewart said he'd give us, if we'd killed you."

"You were given five hundred dollars?"

"No, he didn't give us nothin'. He said he was afraid we'd run off with the money, so he said he wouldn't pay us until after you was killed."

"Well, it looks like you two men came out on the short end of the rope," Lucas said."

"La Cuesta," Taylor said, the word barely heard because Taylor's rapidly deteriorating condition.

"What?"

"La Cuesta...that's where you'll find the son of a bitch."

"Are you talking about Stewart?" Lucas asked.

Lucas's question went unanswered, because Taylor was dead.

LATER ON THAT NIGHT, some thirty miles east of Oje de la Vaca, Dudley Stewart, Sam Coker, Hoot Calhoun, Herman Owens, and Pete Bundy were having their supper. They were gathered in a little two-room shack, two miles west of the village of La Cuesta.

"What do you think about Taylor and Crowley?" Bundy asked. "You think they got Cain?"

"No, 'cause if they did, we'd know about it by now," Stewart said. "Like as not, they got theirselves kilt."

"So then, you give 'em five hunnert dollars for nothin'?" Calhoun asked.

Stewart chuckled. "No, they got theirselves kilt for nothin'. I didn't give 'em no money, and warn't goin' to, 'til they got the job done."

"Maybe we should 'a got somebody else to do it," Bundy suggested.

"Or do it ourselves," Owens said.

"Huh, uh," Bundy said. "I don't want to take no chances with 'im."

"You know what I think, Bundy?" Owens said. "I think Cain has you so a' scairt that you're 'bout to pee in your pants. You goin' to eat the rest of them beans?" Owens raked the rest of Bundy's beans onto his own plate.

"Are you tellin' me you ain't none a'feard o' Cain?" Bundy asked.

"Maybe a little scairt, but there ain't nothin' I can do about it, 'n I ain't goin to sit around cryin' about it. Damn, your beans don't taste no better 'n mine did," Owens said.

"What the hell, did you think they come from a different can?" Bundy asked with a little chuckle.

Calhoun glanced over toward Stewart. "Hey, when are we goin' to get to spend some of this money we got? I'd like to go to town 'n maybe buy me a steak, some taters, 'n some beer. 'N maybe even a woman. Hell, mostly a woman."

"We can't do it yet, Cain's too close on our tail," Stewart said.

"What if we go someplace where he's already been?" Calhoun asked.

"Where he's already been? What are you talkin' about?"

"Well, s'pose we go to that little town where we set Taylor 'n Crowley on 'im? Cain has either done kilt the two of them, 'n has gone on, or they kilt 'im 'n he's already dead, 'n we'll owe Taylor and Crowley five hunnert dollars."

Stewart chuckled. "Yeah, you just might have somethin' there. In the meantime, what do you say we go into town here, 'n blow off a little steam?"

"Sounds good to me," Calhoun said. "When are we goin' to do it?"

"How 'bout first thing tomorrow mornin'?" Stewart suggested.

"I'll be ready," Calhoun replied.

"No readier than I'll be," Bundy added.

"I'm tryin' to make up my mind," Owens said.

"You mean you ain't made up your mind yet whether you even want to go in to town?" Coker asked.

A broad smile spread across Owens's face. "No, I'm tryin' to make up my mind what I want first. Will it be a steak, a beer, or a woman?"

BACK IN OJE de la Vaca, Lucas, now with fresh bandages on the wound in his side, collected the rewards offered for Taylor and Crowley, two hundred and fifty dollars for each of them, then he stopped by the marshal's office to talk to Cletus Moore, who had been Cox's deputy. Moore was a young man, in his early twenties.

"How are you holding out?" Lucas asked.

"I...uh, don't mind telling you, Marshal, that I'm having a hard time," Moore said. "Vernon was more like my dad, than he was my boss."

"I only recently met him," Lucas said, "but he came across as a good man."

"What are you goin' to do now?" Moore asked.

"Taylor gave me a lead on Stewart, so I'm going to follow it up and see where it takes me."

"Are you sure you can trust him?"

"Well, he was literally dying, and he told me with his last breath, so I don't know why he would lie about it."

"You sure you don't want to stick around?" Moore asked. "I know damn well the city council would be willing to appoint you as marshal to take Vernon's place."

"What about you?" Lucas asked. "Surely you can do the job, or Cox would never have made you his deputy in the first place. You do think you can handle it, don't you?"

"Yeah, sure I can. But I'm pretty young, and I just don't know what the folks of the town will think of it," Moore said.

Lucas chuckled, and then reached out to put his hand on Moore's shoulder. "You'll do fine, young man. You'll do just fine."

17

After eating and whoring in La Cuesta, Stewart, Coker, Bundy, Owens and Calhoun went to Oje de la Vaca. It was mid-afternoon by the time they got there. They rode right down the middle of the street with their hands close to their guns, ready at a moment's notice to react to anyone who might challenge them. There were several people in town, crowding the board-walks and the street, but nobody seemed to be paying any attention to Stewart and the others. It was almost as if they hadn't been noticed.

"They's somethin' strange goin' on here," Stewart said. "It's almost like there ain't no one what's even seen us."

"Yeah, well, that there's prob'ly why they ain't nobody payin' no attention to us," Bundy said. "Look down there, they's somethin' that's drawed ever' ones attention."

A large group of people were gathered at the other end of the street, and they all appeared to be looking at something.

"What say we mosey on down there 'n take us a look see?" Stewart suggested.

They rode on down the crowded street toward the gathering, totally unnoticed by any of the citizens of the town. Then, when they drew close enough, they saw what was holding the attention of the crowd.

"Son of a bitch! Look at that!" Owens said, pointing.

It wasn't necessary for Owens to point; the objects of everyone's attention could be clearly seen. There were three coffins standing up against the front window of the hardware store. The coffin lids were not in place, so that the bodies could be clearly seen. One of the bodies had been dressed in a suit, and it was obvious that he had been prepared for burial. There had been no preparation for the other two men, and the bloodstains indicated that they were still in the same clothes they had been wearing when they were killed.

There were signs over the coffins. The sign over the man who was wearing a suit read:

MARSHAL VERNON COX
Killed in the line of duty
A Brave Man

There was only one sign over the other two coffins.

The Outlaws Taylor and Crowley
No first names needed
They are neither mourned nor missed.

"Well, I reckon that tells us that them two men didn't earn their money," Coker said.

"Damn, Stewart, look at that," Owens said, pointing

to a third sign that was in the window of the hardware store.

Dudley Stewart
You're next
Lucas Cain

"Yeah? Well the son of bitch won't get me if we get him first," Stewart said.

The five men rode on through the town then stopped in front of the saloon.

Sofia started toward the front door to welcome the men who had just come in. Then, seeing that one of the men had the deformed eye that Lucas had spoken of, she stopped and took a short, audible breath.

"Well, hello, darlin'," one of the men said, displaying a mouth full of crooked, yellow teeth when he smiled. "How 'bout you come have a drink with us."

"I, uh..." Sofia started, then she realized that if she didn't have a drink with them, they might get a little mean. She forced a smile. "*Si, Señor,* I will drink with you."

"Calhoun, grab a bottle and some glasses," Stewart said. "We'll be over there." He pointed to a table in the back corner.

"I will get my own drink, *Señor,*" Sofia said.

"If we're buyin' the drink, you'll drink what we buy," Stewart said.

"But, *Señor,* I cannot drink whiskey. It will make me sick."

"All right, get your own drink," Stewart said.

THE TOWN of La Cuesta was even smaller than Oje de la Vaca. Lucas saw a small, white building that said "Marshal's Office" so he headed there where he dismounted, and tied Charley II off at the hitching rail in front. When he went into the marshal's office, he saw that it was also a jail, as there was a single cell in the back. The cell was empty and the door open.

The marshal was a thin man with a long, narrow nose, high cheekbones, and brown eyes. He was sitting at his desk, reading a newspaper, and he looked up when Lucas stepped into the room.

"You aren't from around here, are you?" the marshal asked.

"No, I'm not."

"What are doin' here?"

"I'm looking for Dudley Stewart."

"Hell, ain't ever' body?" the city marshal replied. "You think he's here, do you?"

"I've been told that he and his gang were here."

"Yeah, well you was told wrong. He ain't in La Cuesta."

"Somewhere nearby then?" Lucas asked.

"Could be. If he is, it ain't none of my business. I'm a town marshal 'n that means I ain't got no—what do you call it—jurisdiction, outside the town limits."

"I realize that your position limits your jurisdiction to the town, but I was hoping you might have heard something."

"Sorry, I can't help you none."

"Is there a saloon in town? Because if there is, I haven't seen one," Lucas asked.

"Yeah, we got one down to the other end of the street.

It's on the left side of the road. The boards it was built with ain't been painted none, 'n some drunk cowboys tore the sign down a month or so ago. Jenkins, that's the feller that owns the place, just ain't got 'round to puttin' up another sign."

Leaving the marshal's office, Lucas rode down to the saloon. As saloons go, it was small, but then the town was small so the customer base was limited. Lucas wanted a beer to cut the trail dust, but he also hoped he would be able to get some information about Stewart and his men.

There were only about ten men in the saloon, three of them standing at the bar, the others at the four tables. There was no piano and no girls, or at least none that were present at the moment.

"What'll it be, stranger?" the bartender asked.

"I'll have a beer."

The bartender drew the beer from a wooden barrel, then put it in front of Lucas.

"You haven't been here before, have you?"

"No, this is my first time."

"Just passing through, are you?"

Lucas had not intended to ask about Stewart, because often the inquiries would be counterproductive. But the bartender had opened the door for him.

"I'm looking for someone," Lucas replied.

"Give me a name," the bartender said. "If he lives here in town or anywhere close, I can most likely tell you where to find him."

"I'm looking for Dudley Stewart."

The expression on the bartender's face hardened. "You're not plannin' on joinin' up with that son of a bitch, are you? He's got enough worthless bastards around him as it is."

Lucas laughed. "I'm glad we share the same opinion of him."

"Harrumph. If you don't like the son of a bitch, why are looking for him?"

"I'm a U.S. Marshal," Lucas said.

"What's it worth to you if I tell you where to find him?"

"Ten dollars now, and if your tip pays off, I'll make it a hundred."

"If you don't find him, I can keep the ten dollars?"

"If it's a valid lead, you can. But if you're just lying for the money, I'll be back."

The bartender chuckled. "Good enough," he said. "From what I've heard, Stewart and the ones with him have been staying in an old miner's cabin about a mile west of here. You can't miss it. It's the only one there."

"Thanks," Lucas said, handing the bartender a ten-dollar gold piece.

Lucas finished his beer, then left the saloon to check on the cabin the bartender had told him about. He rode by it as if he were just a traveler passing by. The cabin looked deserted, so he decided he would study it for a while. He found a trail that led up to the top of a bluff that allowed him to look down on the cabin.

Lucas watched the cabin until late in the day, but saw no activity. Then, as the sun was setting in the west, he walked out to the edge of the bluff where he looked out over the surrounding countryside.

Lucas decided he may as well spend the night up here, and give it at least one more day of keeping a lookout. So, turning away from the edge of the bluff, he walked back to his horse, untied the bedroll, then took off his pistol belt and hung it from the saddle horn.

"I'll loosen the saddle for you, Charley, but I think it

might be better if I leave it on. There's a little grass here for you to munch on, not much I'll admit, but my supper is only going to be a couple of pieces of jerky, so we're in the same boat."

After Lucas had his supper, he spread out his bedroll, then lay down and looked up at the stars. It didn't take too long for him to go to sleep.

As soon as Stewart and the others with him returned to La Cuesta, they were approached by a man named Jasper Caldwell.

"There's a fella by the name of Lucas Cain that's here, lookin' for you,"

"How do you know he's here?" Stewart asked.

"I know 'cause I heard him 'n Jenkins talkin' about it in the saloon. He give Jenkins ten dollars, 'n Jenkins told 'im 'bout the cabin."

"You're a good man, Caldwell," Stewart said.

"Ten dollars good?"

"How about I just don't shoot you good?"

"I, uh, thought..." Caldwell started.

"You thought what?"

"I, uh, thought I should tell you because it was a friendly thing for me to do."

"Well, good for you," Stewart said.

"What are we going to do, Dudley?" Bundy asked.

"We're going to surprise Mr. Cain," Stewart replied.

"You think he'll be waitin' in the cabin?"

"No, I think he'll be keepin' an eye on it, waiting to see if we come back."

"Where do think he'll be?"

"My guess is he'll be up on the mesa," Stewart said.

18

Lucas was awakened early the next morning by a series of whickers and snorts from his horse. He didn't get up right away, but instead studied the stars which were still visible in the pre-dawn darkness. However, in the east a bar of pearl gray light presaged the coming day. The wind, which had moaned all night long, was quiet now, and a pre-dawn stillness had taken its place. The only sound was the rippling flow of water from the stream below the Mesa.

Awake now, Lucas picked up his bedroll, and walked over to tie it behind the cantle. His pistol belt was still hanging from the saddle horn, and he started to put it on, but decided to have his breakfast first, so he pulled out a piece of jerky, took a bite, then wrapped it up and put it back in the saddle bag. That would have to do him for now.

Again, his horse whickered.

"What's the matter with you, Charley? Why are you carrying on so?"

Then a feeling of foreboding came over Lucas. His

first thought was to go for his pistol, but it was still hanging from the saddle horn, and would be an awkward draw. Also, just as he sensed he was being watched, he knew also that there were guns pointed at him.

"Turn around, you son of a bitch," a low, menacing voice demanded.

"And do it slow," another voice added, giving credence to Lucas's thought that there was more than one gun on him.

"With your hands up," a third voice added.

Lucas turned around, but he could see nothing in the pre-dawn darkness. Then, five men appeared in the gloom. They were walking toward him, all holding guns, and all guns were pointed toward Lucas.

"Well now, lookie here, boys," Stewart said. "This here feller has been lookin' for us, but we found him."

Coker laughed. "Yeah, now ain't this somethin'?"

"We was lookin' for you, 'n heard your horse whickerin' 'n stampin' around," Bundy said.

"Yeah, you'd think a smart man like you would have a horse that would know better," Calhoun added.

"I seen the sign you left for me," Stewart said. "The one that you left in the winder of the hardware store sayin' you was comin' after me."

"Did you, now?" Lucas asked, speaking for the first time.

"Yeah, I seen it. I didn't like it all that much." Stewart laughed. "But to tell the truth, I don't like *you* all that much. You been ridin' my trail pretty hard, 'n I'm gettin' damn tired of it."

"Well, Stewart, I'm an officer of the law, and that's what I do," Lucas said calmly.

"Yeah, well, you don't do it all that well, do you?"

Stewart asked with a little laugh. "I mean, you lookin' for us, 'n here, we found you. Now, that's a little like a rabbit findin' the hound that's a' chasin' it, ain't it, now?"

"I guess you could say that," Lucas answered.

"I'm plannin' on killin' you, you know," Stewart said. "I been payin' folks to have you kilt, but they ain't none of 'em been able to get the job done. So, I guess it's like they say, if you want somethin' done right, do it yourself. Talkin's over now. Come on, boys, let's shoot the son of a bitch 'n be done with it."

During all the time Stewart was talking, Lucas was thinking. He had not seen the five men until they were right on him, because they had approached him from the darkness. On the other hand, they had been able to see him because he was silhouetted against the sky behind him. Lucas realized that if he could just take a couple of steps to his right, he would have the darkness of the mountains behind him. But he needed an edge.

Lucas started to his left, and all five of the outlaws started firing. But even as they were shooting, Lucas had already leaped back to his right, to disappear into the dark maw.

The muzzle flashes of all the guns firing had the effect of temporarily causing night blindness in the shooters.

"Where is he?" Stewart shouted. "Where did the son of a bitch go?"

"I can't see a damn thing," Calhoun said.

"Shoot! Shoot!" Stewart ordered, and the guns fired a second time, even though they still had no idea where Lucas was. Again, the guns lit up the darkness, while intensifying the night blindness.

As Stewart and the others were firing blindly, Lucas had run through the darkness to the edge of the bluff, then he leaped down into the black maw. He knew that there was a steam of water there, and he was just taking a chance that it was close enough. Would it be a bloody and painful death on the rocks, or the relative safety of the water? His stomach leaped into his throat as he plummeted down to whatever awaited him below.

A second later the question was answered as he hit the water, and went under. His desperate gamble had paid off. There were no rocks, only the welcoming embrace of the water. He was safe.

"WHERE'D HE GO?" Bundy shouted.

"I think the son of a bitch went over the edge," Owens said.

The five men ran to the edge of the mesa, and started shooting into the darkness below. As before, the muzzle flashes lit up the nearby trees while burnt powder and acrid smoke drifted up into their faces.

"Stop shootin', stop shootin'! We ain't doin' nothin' but wastin' bullets here," Stewart ordered.

The men stopped shooting as the sounds of the last few rounds fired echoed back to them.

"How far down do you reckon that is?" Coker asked.

"It's at least a hunnert feet down there," Calhoun said.

"Hell, that son of a bitch is dead, kilt when he hit them rocks."

"I'll throw a rock over," Owens said, picking up a stone and tossing it over. The five men listened closely.

"Hell, that rock ain't hit yet," Owens said. He laughed. "Yes, sir, that son of a bitch is dead, sure as hell."

"Kill his horse," Stewart said.

"What for do you want to kill his horse?" Coker

asked.

"Just in case that fall didn't kill 'im," Stewart said. "I want him to be on foot."

"Yeah, that's prob'ly a good idea," Coker said. "I'll do it."

Coker walked over to Lucas's horse with his pistol drawn, but Charley II, sensing something was wrong, jerked his head up, pulling himself free from the ground hobble. That same action pushed Coker away from him, throwing Coker off balance, and Charley II galloped away.

"Hey, come back here!" Coker called.

"Stewart, the horse is getting away!" Bundy shouted.

"Shoot 'im!" Stewart ordered, and all five men began blazing away at the galloping horse. But they were no luckier in shooting the horse, than they had been in trying to shoot Lucas. Within a moment, the only sign of the horse was the sound of his retreating hoof beats as he galloped away.

"He got away," Coker said.

"I can see that, you dumbass. I should have done it myself," Stewart said.

"Yeah, well, I don't see any difference that it makes whether the horse got away or not," Calhoun said. "You know damn well Cain is deader 'n hell."

"We're goin' to find out for sure whether he's dead or not," Stewart said. "Come daylight, we're goin' to climb down there 'n take us a look see."

"Now, why the hell do we want to do that?" Owens asked. "We'll just be wastin' our time. We know damn well, he's dead."

"I'd just like to make sure," Stewart said.

Lucas let the current carry him at least half-a-mile downstream, being swept painfully through rapids and across rocks before he decided to come out. By the time he decided to leave the Rio Pecos, he had so many cuts and bruises that he didn't know which ones were new and which ones were old.

Lucas swam toward the riverbank, then grabbed an overhanging tree branch to pull himself from the water. Slowly and painfully he crawled away until he was on flat ground, and there he lay on his back exhausted from the efforts, and shaking with the cold.

Although it seemed as if Lucas had only closed his eyes for a moment, when he opened them again the sun was high, and his clothes were dry. He heard a whickering sound and when he looked around, he was shocked to see Charley II calmly cropping grass, no more than ten yards away. His pistol belt still hung from the saddle horn and his rifle was still in the saddle sheath. He hadn't lost a thing.

"Charley!" Lucas called out, excitedly. Charley lifted his head and turned to look at him.

Cautiously, Lucas got to his feet, then walked over to put his arms around Charley's neck. "Charley, my boy, I don't know how the hell you got here, but I'm damn glad you did."

Because the cabin where they were living had been compromised, Stewart made the decision to move on. Now, he was standing at a rock on top of the pass, looking back toward the way they had come. From here, he could see several miles in any direction and he stood there for a spell, just perusing the area. They had stopped when they reached the top, ostensibly to give their horses a breather. But in reality, Stewart just wanted to make sure they weren't being followed.

Behind Stewart, his men were being entertained by a show of marksmanship from Sam Coker. The sound of pistol shots rolled down the mountainside, then picked up resonance to be echoed back from the neighboring mountains. Coker poked out the empty shell casings, then starting shoving new bullets in the cylinder chambers. He looked back at the others with a satisfied smile on his face.

"I'd like to see any of you match that," Coker said with an arrogant sneer.

"Yeah, Coker, you're pretty damn good all right," Calhoun said. "Better 'n any of us, I reckon. But you might have noticed that what you was shootin' at was a whiskey bottle. 'N here's the thing about whiskey bottles that maybe you wasn't thinkin' about. They don't shoot back."

"What the hell does that mean, they don't shoot back?"

"Well, let's say that instead of shootin' at whisky bottles, you was a' shootin' at Lucas Cain. Iffen that's what you was doin', why, ole' Cain will be shootin' back. You can count on that."

"What are you talkin' about? Hell, Cain is dead. We all seen 'im go over the edge of the mesa."

"That's just the thing. When we clumb down there to find his body, he was gone."

"That don't mean nothin'. Like as not he was able to crawl over to the water, 'n got his ass swept down river. Hell, some prospector will find him in the next week or two, deader 'n a doornail." Coker laughed. "Or it might be that someone could find his bones a hunnert years or so from now, 'n they'll be wondering just how the hell that skeleton got there."

Bundy laughed. "Yeah, he's dead, that's for sure."

"No, he ain't dead," Owens said. Owens pulled his pistol, then fired at the whiskey bottle that had been Coker's target, breaking the last piece of glass. "I don't think he's dead, 'n neither does Stewart."

"What makes you think Stewart don't believe he's dead?" Bundy asked.

"Why do you think he's been standing over there, lookin' back from where we come?"

Stewart climbed down from the rock then came over to the others, glaring at them with the indirect stare caused by his bad eye.

"Calhoun's right," Stewart said. "Cain ain't dead. He's still back there, still lookin' for me."

"How do you know he ain't dead?" Coker asked. "Did you see him?"

"No, I didn't see him, but I can feel him," Stewart replied.

"Dudley, you said we would kill him, then we wouldn't have nothin' to worry about," Bundy said.

"I have to confess, I ain't never run across no one nor nothin' that took as much killin' as Lucas Cain does," Stewart said.

"Well, I ain't a' waitin' around no more," Bundy said.

"What do you mean, you ain't waitin' around no more?" Calhoun asked.

"I mean I'm runnin' from him."

Stewart laughed. "Well, now, Pete, how 'bout you tellin' us where you're runnin' to get away from Cain, 'cause if you know of such a place, we'll all just go with you. Don't you understand? We ain't exactly invitin' the son of a bitch to a sit down dinner. It's just that there don't seem like there's no place we can go where he can't find us."

"What if we split up?" Calhoun asked.

"Yeah, that makes a lot of sense," Coker said. "That way he can kill us one at a time."

"Listen, there's a nice, fat bank over in Pecos," Stewart said. "I wouldn't be surprised if they didn't have at least ten thousand dollars just a' sittin' there. We could hit it 'n it'd give us two thousand dollars apiece. With that much money we could take a train to San Francisco, or Denver, or even Kansas City. We'd be so far away from Cain then, that he'd never find us, 'n we could live just fine on all that money for a long time."

"That sounds good to me," Bundy said.

"Yeah, me, too," Owens said.

"I'm all for it," Coker added.

Calhoun was the only one who didn't respond to Stewart's suggestion.

"Hoot, we ain't heard nothin' from you," Stewart said. "Are you with us, or not?"

"Yeah, I'm with the rest of you," Calhoun replied. "But if you don't mind, I'll just meet you fellers in Pecos. I think I'd rather travel by myself for a while."

"No, meet us in El Pueblo. I don't want no one in Pecos until we're ready to hit the bank."

"All right, El Pueblo."

"Have it your way," Stewart said. "But if you ain't there when we go in, you don't get none of the money."

"I'll be there."

LUCAS HAD JUST LEANED over to rub his horse behind the ear, because he knew that Charley II liked that. That little act of kindness saved his life, because he heard the crack of a rifle, and the sound of a bullet whizzing by where he had been but a second earlier.

Lucas jerked his horse around, and drawing his pistol, galloped toward the little whiff of smoke, some one hundred yards away. The gun smoke was drifting up from behind a boulder, and Lucas knew that if his assailant was going to take a second shot, he would have to raise up to aim, and if he did so at this range, Lucas could put a bullet right between the shooter's eyes.

When Lucas reached the knoll, he leaped down from the saddle, and pulling his horse behind the knoll and out the line of fire, he crawled up to a rock and looked toward the boulder from where the shot had come.

From here, he had an excellent view and he saw a flash of light, which was the sun's reflection on the spent brass casing that had been ejected from the rifle after the shot had been fired. That was all he could see, so he lay there for several minutes looking for a person, but saw no one.

"What do you think, Charley?" Lucas said, speaking to his horse. "I think we may have scared him away. The question is, was that Dudley Stewart, or one of the men he has with him?"

Lucas saw the tracks of his would-be ambusher, so he began following them. His quarry made every effort to elude him, from riding over rocks to tying a branch to the tail of his horse in an effort to wipe out his tracks. Despite his determination to destroy his trail, Lucas managed to stick with him. He knew that he could, quite easily overtake the man he was following, but he didn't do so, because he hoped the trail would lead him to Dudley Stewart and all the men who were riding with him.

Shortly after nightfall, Lucas saw a campfire ahead. He was confused by the sight. It didn't seem likely to Lucas that the man he was trailing who had made every effort to cover his trail, would have a campfire to give away his position. Of course, the fire could also be bait to draw Lucas in and make a target of him. Considering that possibility, Lucas approached the campfire slowly, and very cautiously.

It was just as Lucas thought. The fire illuminated an empty campsite.

Lucas continued on, until he came to a very steep hill, covered with sharp rocks. It was too dangerous to try and climb in the dark, so he decided to make his camp here for the rest of the night.

SOMETHING AWAKENED LUCAS, though there had been no noise. It was just a feeling that interrupted his sleep. Lucas had no idea what time it was, but he figured it must be somewhere between two and three in the morning. Leaving his bed roll, Lucas stayed low to the ground and moved over to a depression, then crawled down into it. Once there, he looked back at the bedroll, and at a not too thorough an examination, it looked like he was still there.

Shortly after Lucas moved back into the depression, his feeling of foreboding was borne out when he saw a muzzle flash, followed by the sound of a rifle shot. Lucas saw a puff of dust from the impact of the bullet striking the blanket of his bedroll. He waited to see if his assailant would follow up on the shot.

There were no more shots and no one appeared. A moment later, Lucas heard the sound of hoofbeats as his attacker rode away. The rider was making a hasty retreat without checking to see whether or not he had killed Lucas. Lucas let him go, thinking that if the shooter believed that Lucas was dead, he might lead him to the others.

Lucas was right. The trail was a lot easier to follow after sunrise, and that proved to be true, because Lucas came within sight of the rider by mid-morning.

CALHOUN GLANCED BACK over his shoulder and was shocked to see that he was being trailed. He urged his horse into a gallop.

WHEN LUCAS SAW his quarry break into a gallop, he urged his own horse forward to keep up. But after a few minutes, he realized that all this was accomplishing, was to run Charley II into the ground. Then he got an idea. They were riding parallel to a long ridge. Whoever he was chasing would have to pass around the ridge at the far end. If Lucas crossed the ridge, he could overtake the rider.

Lucas urged Charley II up the ridge, but when he got to the top, he saw that a gulley on the other side would take away any advantage he might have had in intercepting him, but it did give him the opportunity for a long-distance shot. He rode to the edge of the ridge, pulled his rifle from the saddle sheath, then waited for the rider to appear.

He saw the rider, who had slowed down now, convinced that he had escaped his pursuer. Lucas lifted one leg, and crossed it on the saddle in front of him, then used it to support his elbow while he took aim. He wasn't aiming at the rider—he was aiming at the horse.

"I'm sorry, horse, it's not your fault that your owner is a son of a bitch," he said quietly. He took a deep breath, let half of it out, held it, then pulled the trigger. He saw the horse stumble forward a few steps, then go down onto his forelegs. That had the effect of throwing his rider over his head, then the horse fell to the ground.

It took Lucas a few minutes to reach the site of the downed horse. His rider was sitting on the ground in front of him, his knees raised, and his arms wrapped around his legs.

"I'm sorry about your horse," Lucas said as he dismounted.

"You're Lucas Cain, ain't you?"

"I am indeed. And what is your name?"

"Calhoun. Hoot Calhoun."

Lucas chuckled. "Well, it's good to know your whole name so I can match you with the paper that's out on you. But I doubt we'll ever get on a first name basis."

"My God, you aren't human," Calhoun said. "Stewart's been trying to get rid of you for a long time now, but there ain't been nobody that's been able to get the job done. Can't you be killed?"

"Of course I can," Lucas said. He pulled his pistol. "And so can you, if you don't come with me now."

"Where we goin'?"

Lucas pointed to the east. "San Jon is about six miles that way. I'm going to leave you in jail there, while I go after the others."

"Yeah? Well now just how in the hell do you expect to get me there? You killed my horse."

"You'll walk."

"Huh, uh," Calhoun said. "I ain't a' goin' to be walkin' no six miles."

"Well, I'll give you your choice. You'll either walk, or I'll hog tie you and drag you."

IT MADE QUITE A SCENE WHEN, an hour and a half later Lucas rode into San Jon with Calhoun, cuffed and being led by a rope, walking behind him.

"Hey, look at that!" someone shouted, pointing toward Lucas and his prisoner.

"That ain't no way to treat a man," another said.

"Mister, what the hell you doin'?" someone shouted.

Lucas paid no attention to the curious and even angry shouts, but continued down the street until he reached the sheriff's office. He dismounted, then shortened the rope preparatory to taking Calhoun into jail, when the sheriff stepped outside, then leaned against the door frame with his arms crossed in front of him.

"Mister, just what in the hell do you think you're doin', bringin' a man in like that, at the end of a rope?"

"I'm bringin' 'im into jail," Lucas said. "Are you the sheriff?"

"Yes, Sheriff Bostic, 'n the only way someone gets put into my jail is if I say they can go there."

"He's a wanted man, Sheriff," Lucas said.

"Yeah? Well he ain't wanted by me. Who is this man, anyway?"

By now many of the townspeople who had watched Lucas and Calhoun come into town, were now gathered around the sheriff's office to watch the drama being played out in front of them.

"His name is Hoot Calhoun, and he's one of Dudley Stewart's gang."

"Dudley Stewart's gang?" one of the onlookers said.

"Dudley Stewart's gang," Sheriff Bostic replied, his face twisted into a shocked expression. "Look here, didn't Stewart get a couple of his men out of jail once, by blowin' it up?"

"I've heard that story," Lucas said. "I don't know it for a fact, though."

"Yeah, well I do know it for a fact, 'n I sure as hell don't plan on gettin' my jail blowed up," Sheriff Bostic said, angrily.

"Sheriff, he's worth two hundred and fifty dollars to me. So, I'll need you to send a wire to wherever you need to authorize you paying the reward for bringing him in. I'll be waiting for the money in the saloon."

"Mister, didn't you hear what I told you?" Sheriff Bostic said, pointing at Calhoun. "This here man ain't goin' to go into my jail, just so's Stewart can come here 'n blow it up so he can get this man...Calhoun is it?"

"Yes, Hoot Calhoun."

"Well, I've no intention of putting Calhoun in jail."

"All right, if that's the way it is, you don't have to put him in jail," Lucas said.

"Well now, thank you, sheriff," Calhoun turned to Lucas. "See there, this nice man doesn't want me. That sort of takes away your plans, don't it?" he said with a cackling laugh.

"I still plan to collect the reward so when you get the authorization for the money, I'll be waiting in the saloon," Lucas said.

"Mister, I'm not telling you again that I don't intend..." Sheriff Bostic stopped when he saw Lucas pull his pistol and put it to Calhoun's head. "Look here, Mister! What are you doing?" he called out, loudly.

"Calhoun is wanted dead or alive," Lucas said easily. "So if you don't want him alive, I'll just kill him. It doesn't make any difference to me. I'll be waiting for my money in the saloon." Lucas cocked his pistol.

Calhoun's eyes opened wide in fear. "Sheriff, can't you see that this man will do what he says? Please, let me stay in your jail! I won't give you no trouble, I promise you," he begged.

"Now you just hold on a minute here, Mister!" the sheriff demanded. "You can't just threaten to blow man's brains out right here in front of the whole town." The sheriff took in the crowd of people who were now watching in shock.

"Oh, I'd say that it's more of a promise than a threat," Lucas said, calmly.

"Just who the hell do you think you are, anyway?" Sheriff Bostic demanded to know.

"The name is Cain. Lucas Cain."

"Lucas Cain!" someone in the crowd gasped, and now the name became a buzzing whisper, repeated many times as, by now, nearly all of them had heard of Lucas Cain.

"Oh," Sheriff Bostic said, the bluster now gone from his voice. "Well, why didn't you say so? I'll be glad to hold your prisoner for you. And I'll pay you the reward as soon as I get it authorized."

"Good," Lucas said, easing the hammer back down and holstering his pistol. "Like I said, I'll be waiting in the saloon. Bring the money over there as soon as it comes in."

"Yes, sir, Mr. Cain, as soon as it comes in," Sheriff Bostic agreed, obsequiously.

19

The saloon, which called itself the Happy Trails Saloon, was one of the nicer ones Lucas had seen in quite a while. The bar was of polished mahogany with brass rings spaced about every four feet on front of the bar, from which hung clean, white towels. There was a mirror behind the bar, flanked on either side by a small statue of a nude woman. The statues were sitting on a shelf, which was itself, set back in a niche. Two, glistening chandeliers hung from the ceiling. At the back of the saloon a broad set of stairs climbed to a second floor. The front part of the second floor was open, which provided a balcony that overlooked the ground floor.

When Lucas stepped up to the bar, the bartender, a middle-aged man with graying hair and a walrus moustache, set down a glass he was polishing and stepped down toward him.

"What'll it be, Mister?"

"Is your beer cold?"

"Colder 'n a glass of piss," the bartender replied.

Lucas smiled. "I reckon that's cold enough. He put a

half-dime on the bar, then picked up the mug of beer the bartender had placed before him. He turned to look out over the floor as he took his first swallow.

There was a piano at the back of the room, and the music the pianist was playing was different from the songs one would hear in most of the saloons.

"What's that he's playing?" Lucas asked the bartender.

"Chopin."

"I've never heard of a song called Chopin, but it's pretty."

The bartender chuckled. "Chopin isn't the name of the song, it's the name of the composer who wrote the song. Professor Collins is what you call a classical pianist, and he has played in the finest concert houses in the world."

"Really?"

"I know what you're going to ask. How did someone like the professor wind up playing a piano in a saloon in a town like San Jon?"

"I was wondering about that, yes."

"His wife left him for some London court dandy. The professor left the concert circuit, took to the bottle, started wandering around, and somehow wound up here. You might call him a rambling man."

"A rambling man. Yes, I can relate to that."

Lucas saw that there were two card games going on, one table had four cowboys who were playing for matches and tobacco. A second table had four men who were playing for money. One of the men who was playing for money, got up and left the table.

"We have an open chair here," one of the remaining players called out. "What about you, Dawes, you want to join us?"

"I can't afford it," one of players at the other table

called back. "I'm playing for matches and tobacco here, and I'm losing."

"I'll join your game, if you don't mind," Lucas said.

"As long as you've got money to play, you're good with us," the man who had issued the invitation replied.

"Hey, don't I know you?" one of the players asked, when Lucas joined the table.

"I don't know," Lucas replied.

"My name is Blake. Steve Blake."

"Sorry, it doesn't ring a bell," Lucas said. He didn't give his own name.

"Hey, Steve, were you down at the sheriff's office with all the others about half-an-hour ago?" one of the players from the matches and tobacco table asked.

"No, should I have been?" Blake asked, counting out twenty dollars' worth of chips for Lucas.

"Well, it's just if you had of been, you would 'a seen that this man brung in the outlaw Hoot Calhoun. The man you're playin' with is Lucas Cain."

Baker ran the back of his finger across his lips, as he considered whether or not someone like Lucas Cain might be too dangerous to play cards with. Then, with a shrug, he decided that since neither he nor either of the other two players was wanted, they would have nothing to fear from him. He shoved the deck of cards across the table.

"Since you're the new player, you can cut the cards," Blake said, handing the deck to Lucas.

Holding the cards, Lucas fanned the deck open and felt for any pinpricks in the back of the cards, then closing the deck he felt around the edge for nicks, or rounded corners. He found nothing amiss, which meant that the deck was honest. It remained to be seen whether or not the players were honest. He cut the deck then handed it back to Blake, who was smiling.

"Fellas, we're playing with a cautious man," he said, as he began to deal.

"SHERIFF? SHERIFF?" Calhoun called from the jail cell. "Sheriff, you out there?"

Sheriff Bostic looked up from his paperwork. "Yeah, I'm here. What do you want?"

"I want a drink of water."

"You'll be getting your supper soon, you'll get water then."

"But I'm thirsty now," Calhoun complained.

"You aren't goin' to die of thirst between now 'n supper."

"Come on Sheriff, that damn Cain made me walk six miles. You seen the way that son of a bitch dragged me in here."

With a sigh, Sheriff Bostic lay the accounts book aside. "All right, I'll get you a drink of water, but then I don't want to hear another word from you until supper. You got that?"

"Yeah, Sheriff, thanks," Calhoun replied.

Sheriff Bostic went to the water bucket, filled the dipper, then took it back to the cell.

Calhoun reached for it.

"Wait, I'll have to tip it slightly to get it between the bars," Bostic said.

"I don't care how you do it, I'm dyin' of thirst here."

Bostic passed the dipper through, and as soon as Calhoun touched it, he tipped the dipper so that all the water spilled onto the sheriff's shirt.

"Damn it, Calhoun, why couldn't you be more careful? Look what you did."

As Bostic was concentrating on his shirt, he was paying no attention to Calhoun who reached through the bars, grabbed the sheriff's hair, then jerking it toward him slammed his head against the bars with a sudden unexpected and powerful move. The sheriff was knocked unconscious and fell to the floor just outside the cell door.

Calhoun squatted down, then reached through the bars to get the ring of keys which the sheriff had attached to his belt. Getting the ring he had to try four keys before he found the one that worked, and using it, he unlocked the cell door. He was a free man.

Once out of the cell, Calhoun hurried over to the sheriff's desk, then began jerking open drawers looking for his pistol and holster.

"Damnit, Sheriff, what the hell did you do with my pistol?" Calhoun asked under his breath. Then, because he was frightened someone might come in and catch him, he gave up looking for his pistol and just grabbed a shotgun off the rack. Breaking it open, he saw that both barrels were charged, so he snapped it shut, then looked over at the sheriff who was still lying on the floor, unconscious.

"It's been nice knowin' you, Sheriff," he said facetiously.

Calhoun let himself out the back door, then started down the alley intending to go to the livery and taking a horse at gunpoint if need be.

As Calhoun walked down the alley he passed by the back end of a saloon. There was no sign, but he was able to identify it by the smell of whiskey and beer.

He stopped for a moment. Cain had told the sheriff

he would be waiting in the saloon, and he was no doubt in there now. How many drinks had he had, Calhoun wondered. Enough to slow him down?

Cain believed that Calhoun was still in jail. There would never be an opportunity like this to settle the score for Cain bringing him in. Hell, Calhoun would be looked at as a hero by the others for taking care of business like this. He saw a set of stairs at the back of the saloon leading up to the second floor. Hell, this was going to be as easy as shooting fish in a barrel.

Calhoun laughed at the idiom. The saloon was the barrel and Lucas Cain was the fish. Looking around to make certain nobody saw him, Calhoun started up the stairs to the second floor.

IN THE SALOON, Lucas was enjoying the game of poker he was playing. He had played enough hands to know that it was an honest game. Whether everyone was honest, or whether they weren't cheating because they were frightened of him, he didn't know, but he appreciated the honesty. Another reason he was enjoying the game was because he was fifty dollars ahead.

"Damn, you won again," Blake said. "I was sure my two pair of Aces and Jacks were enough to win. But no, you had to have three sevens."

"I tell you what," Lucas said. "If it'll make you men feel better about it, I'll buy a round of drinks for the table."

"It'll help," McCoy, one of the other players said, with a little chuckle.

Lucas excused himself, and stepped over to the bar.

"Bartender, if I bought four drinks for the table and a

drink for one of these pretty young ladies you've got workin' here, do you think she would help me get the drinks over to the table?"

"Why don't you ask Katie, there?" the bartender said with a nod toward the girl who was standing close enough to them to have overheard the question.

"Honey, I'll be glad to take your drinks over to the table for you," Katie said with a pretty and seductive smile.

As the bartender was drawing the four mugs of beer, Lucas got a strong feeling of foreboding. This was a sixth sense that those who 'live on the edge' often develop, and it had saved Lucas's life often enough that he never ignored it.

Looking in the mirror, he saw someone up on the balcony holding a shotgun. At first, the man was in the shadows, but as he stepped out of the shadows and up to the rail, Lucas could see his face. The face, which was wearing a broad, triumphant smile, was that of Hoot Calhoun.

"Bartender, get down!" Lucas shouted, while at the same time pushing Katie away.

Katie had no idea what was going on, but his strange actions frightened her, and she hurried to get away from the bar.

Lucas's shout, and his strange action of pushing the girl away got the attention of everyone else in the saloon, and all conversation ceased as they looked up to see Lucas draw his pistol.

"Cain, you son of a bitch, I'm going to kill you!" Calhoun shouted from the overlook balcony.

The shotgun boomed as soon as he said the words.

Lucas had moved away from the bar as he was

drawing his pistol, and was pulling the trigger, even as the shotgun boomed.

The heavy charge of the shotgun blew a huge hole in the bar where, but a moment earlier, Lucas and Katie had been standing. Some of the shot hit the whiskey bottles and the mirror behind the bar. Pieces of glass flew everywhere. The mirror fell, except for the jagged shards which remained. Those shards reflected half a dozen images of the drama that was playing out before them.

Lucas's shot had been more accurately placed, and Calhoun's eyes opened wide as he dropped the shotgun and grabbed his neck. Blood spilled between his fingers. He twisted around and fell on his back, then slid head-first down the stairs, following the clattering shotgun. When he reached the ground floor, he lay motionless on the bottom step, his neck and shirt covered with blood and his eyes open and sightless.

Even before the gun smoke rolled away, Sheriff Bostic was pushing his way through the swinging doors of the saloon. His hair was matted with blood and his pistol was in his hand. He stopped just inside the door and looked around to study the situation.

"It was self-defense, Sheriff," Blake called out. "That fella lyin' at the foot of the stairs, there, threw down on Cain with a shotgun."

"Yeah, I know," Sheriff Bostic answered. "That would be my shotgun Calhoun was using." Bostic holstered his pistol, and Lucas put his own gun away. "I'm ashamed to say that the son of a bitch tricked me and got away. Are you all right, Cain?"

"Yeah, thanks."

Bostic walked over to look down at Calhoun's body. Lucas, and some of the other saloon patrons, joined him.

"It's a funny thing," the sheriff said.

"What's funny?"

"Why did he come in here to try and kill you? I mean, he got away from the jail. If he had just kept going, he would've got away. Instead, he came in here to kill you. He would be free by now."

"No, he wouldn't," Lucas answered.

"What do you mean, he wouldn't."

"I would have found him, and brought him in. Just like I'm going to do with Stewart and the others."

Bostic looked at Lucas and shook his head. "I sure as hell hope you don't ever come after me."

Lucas chuckled. "Well, Sheriff, if you don't ever get any dodgers out with your name on them, I won't."

Bostic chuckled as well, then looked over at some of the others who had gathered around to look down at the body. "How 'bout a couple of you men get this body down to the undertaker? There's five dollars in it for you."

"The reward money here yet?" Lucas asked.

"I'll go down to the Western Union and check. Authorization should be here by now."

"Good, I'd like to get the money and be gone."

"Hey, Cain, how 'bout those drinks you promised us?" Blake called.

"Yeah, we never did get those, did we?"

"Katie," Lucas said with a smile. "Serve my friends, would you?"

"Yes, sir, Mr. Cain," Katie replied, nervously.

For a moment, Lucas wondered why Katie had replied in such a way, then he remembered that it had been necessary for him to push her away. He didn't join the others, but picked up his own beer at the counter, and watched as they took Calhoun's body away.

The sheriff started to leave, then he looked back toward Lucas.

"Look, I'm sorry 'bout this, Cain. I should have been paying more attention to what I was doing, than to let him pull a stunt on me like that."

"Yeah, well, don't worry about it, Sheriff. It looks to me like I could have saved everyone a lot of trouble if I had just gone ahead and blown his brains out like I started to."

"Would you really have done that, Cain?"

Lucas took a swallow of his beer, then smiled before he answered. "Do you play poker, Sheriff?"

"Yeah, sure."

"Then, you don't really expect me to answer that question, do you?"

20

Dudley Stewart and the others were in the Horseshoe Saloon in El Pueblo, New Mexico. They were waiting there for Calhoun, who had told them when they separated, that he would meet them here.

"Where the hell is Calhoun?" Stewart asked, his voice clearly showing his agitation. "He was supposed to have joined up with us by now."

"Maybe he's plannin' to meet us in Pecos," Coker suggested.

"I sure as hell hope not. That's all we need…some fool wanderin' around the streets askin' about us in the same town where we're plannin' to rob a bank," Stewart said. "If we're goin' to do a proper job o' robbin' the bank, we got to go in unnoticed."

"You shouldn't 'a let 'im ride off by his ownself," Owens said.

"I didn't have much choice," Stewart replied. "You seen how jumpy he was. We don't need nobody around us as jumpy as all that."

"Ha! If I know old Hoot, he's somewhere gettin' his wick dipped," Sam Coker said.

"There'll be time for that after we hit the bank," Stewart said.

"You want me to go back 'n see if I can find 'im?" Coker asked.

"Yeah," Stewart answered. "And when you find 'im, tell 'im if he wants a share of this money, he'd better get his ass up here, damn soon."

"All right," Coker agreed. "It might take me two or three days."

"No more than three days. When you find 'im, meet up with us at El Pueblo on Thursday. That's just a little over ten miles west of where we'll be hitting the bank."

"All right," Coker said.

"Wait a minute," Stewart called, as Coker stood up from the table where they were all sitting. "It could be that the dumb son of a bitch has got hisself caught, 'n is in jail."

"If he's in jail, I'm not sure I could break him out, not all by myself, anyway," Coker said.

"I don't want you to try and break 'im out," Stewart said. "If he's in jail, I want you to kill 'im."

"Kill 'im? Look here, Dudley, are you sure about that? Do you really want me to kill 'im?" Coker replied, clearly shocked by the suggestion.

"I wouldn't have said it, if I didn't mean it."

"But Hoot's been with us from the very beginning," Coker said. "I thought we was all friends."

"We work together, we ain't all friends. 'N you know as well as I do, that if they start puttin' any pressure on Calhoun, he'll start spilling his guts. No, sir, if he's in jail, 'bout the only thing we can do, is kill 'im."

"Coker, you know Dudley's right about that," Owens

said. "If Hoot's in jail, the moment they put any pressure on 'im he'll start blabberin' away about the bank job we'll be pullin' in Pecos 'n the next thing you know, we'll have a posse waitin' there to meet us."

"Hell, if he don't want to do it, I will," Bundy volunteered. "I never liked that snivelin', cowardly bastard nohow."

"I'll do it," Coker said.

Fifteen minutes later, after Coker had left on his mission to find Calhoun, Owens raised a question. "Hey, Stewart, what if Calhoun and Coker both don't show up on Thursday?"

"We'll do the job ourselves."

"But that means there'll only be three of us."

Stewart smiled. "Ten thousand dollars goes a lot further split three ways, than it does five ways, or even four ways."

"Yeah," Owens said with a big grin. "Yeah, I like that. I hope neither one of the sons of bitches show up."

LUCAS SAT on the bank of the Rio Pecos River with his boots off and his feet in the water. He had come back to the river because this is where he had last encountered Stewart and the others, and he was hoping he would find some sign. It was getting late, so he thought he might spend the night here. There was certainly an ample supply of water, and there was a channel that cut back into the mesa which would allow him to have a campfire so he could cook the rabbit he had shot a little earlier. Rabbit and beans would be considerably more appetizing than jerky and beans.

If he couldn't pick up any useable sign by noon

tomorrow, he would ride into the nearest town and start asking questions. He knew that Stewart liked his pleasures, and that would require civilization. Maybe he would get lucky.

After supper that night, Lucas made certain that Charley II was tethered, then he threw out his bedroll, and went to sleep.

The nightmare didn't come until later.

It was two o'clock in the morning and the boat was struggling against the surging current of the Mississippi River eight miles north of Memphis, Tennessee, when suddenly one of the boilers exploded. The boat was ripped in half by the explosion, which also ignited flames and released scalding steam.

Lucas was sleeping on the after-hurricane deck and awakened to the gruesome scene of bodies, along with metal fragments from the boilers, splintered wood and other debris raining down on the boat and into the water.

One of the two boat chimneys came crashing down on the hurricane deck, killing many.

Lucas called for his friend, telling him they had to get off the boat, but his friend was trapped under the chimney.

As Lucas strained to free his friend from the fallen chimney, he could hear others screaming in terror and pain.

Finally, Lucas chopped away enough of the chimney debris that he was able to free his friend.

"Come on, we've got to get off this boat!" Lucas shouted.

When Lucas hit the water, the cold took his breath away. The Sultana was near mid-channel and it was over a mile to either side of the river. He was certain he was going to drown.

LUCAS WOKE UP THEN, gasping for breath. It had been a nightmare, but it was a nightmare with substance, because Lucas actually had been on the Sultana when it sank. The riverboat was carrying home men who had been prisoners of war of the Confederacy when the boilers exploded, taking 1,169 lives.

Breakfast was left-over rabbit and coffee, then Lucas saddled Charley II and continued his search for Stewart and the others. He wasn't sure of the names of the others, or even how many there were. He did know that Sam Coker was one of the men who rode with Stewart.

After an all-day ride, the night creatures had begun their evening serenade as Lucas stood on a hill and looked down on the little town of La Cuesta. A cloud passed over the moon then moved on, painting the little town below him in hues of silver and black. From here, it was easy to locate the cantina, because it was the biggest and most brightly lit building in the entire town.

Remounting, Lucas rode down the hill and into the town. As he drew closer, he could hear music coming from the cantina. Someone was playing a guitar, and whoever it was, was quite good. The music spilled out in a steady beat with two or three minor chords at the end of each phrase. A single string melody worked its way in and out of the chords like a thread of gold, woven through the finest cloth. Lucas liked this kind of music. It was mournful and lonesome, the kind of a melody a man could let run through his mind on the long, quiet rides.

It had been four days since Lucas had killed Calhoun, and Stewart's trail had gone cold on him. He knew only that Stewart and his men had been heading in this general direction, and they may be here now. If not, there was the possibility that they had been here, and he might be able to get a lead by talking to some of the people in the cantina. The only way to find out would be to go into the cantina and, maybe, question a few people. At the very least, he could enjoy a beer.

As he rode into the town, he could hear the sounds of civilization. A dog barked, a baby cried, and a Mexican housewife let forth with a long string of Spanish invectives. He caught the aroma of spicy beans and beef coming from one of the houses, and he looked forward to the supper he would buy in one of the restaurants, after he had his beer.

Dismounting in front of the cantina, Lucas tethered Charley II to the hitching rail, then stepped inside. He went to the far end of the bar then around the curve of the bar so that his back was to the wall, and he was facing the door. The bartender, with dark hair, a dark moustache, brown eyes, and swarthy skin, moved down the bar to address him.

"Si, Señor?"

"Do you have beer?"

"No, *Señor*. We have only tequila."

"That'll do."

Lucas put a coin on the bar. He had quite a bit of money now, more than he liked to carry, but he had the two-hundred-fifty-dollar reward money, plus the fifty dollars he had won in the card game.

"Tell me, is there a hotel in town?" Lucas asked

"*Si*, there is one next door. You can also take your meal there."

There was a young boy sweeping the floor, and Lucas called out to him.

"Boy, my horse is tied up out front." Lucas gave him a dollar. "Put him up at the livery. When that is done, come see me at the hotel."

"Si, Señor," the boy replied.

There was a restaurant in the front of the hotel, and Lucas ordered steak and eggs. The boy came to see him before he was finished eating.

"Your horse is put up, *Señor,*" the boy said.

"Good, thank you. Would you like to eat supper with me?"

"*Señor,* I do not have the money for such a fine meal."

Lucas called the waitress over and ordered another meal of steak and eggs."

"Muchas gracias, Senor."

21

Sam Coker had been sent by Stewart to find out why Calhoun hadn't joined them. Then, discovering that Calhoun had been killed in a shootout with Lucas Cain, he was on his way back to report what he had discovered. It was quite late when he rode into the little town of La Cuesta. His first stop was the cantina. He had no idea that Lucas Cain was in town, but he learned that fact because he overheard the bartender talking to one of his customers.

"*Si*, there is a U.S. Marshal here. His name is Lucas Cain."

"What's that? Lucas Cain did you say? Is he still here, or has he left town?" Coker asked.

"Oh, he has not left town, *Señor*. We are very honored that he is still here. He has taken a room in our hotel. Why do you ask about him? Is he your amigo?"

"Uh, yeah, Cain is a friend of mine."

The coin Coker had used to pay for his drink was still lying on the bar, and the bartender put his finger on it, then slid it back across the bar to Coker.

"You must be a good man to have Lucas Cain as your amigo. Your drink will cost you nothing."

"Really?" Coker said, picking up the coin and putting it back in his pocket. He laughed. "Now, that's a pretty good joke on old Cain. Yes, sir, that's a damn good joke."

AFTER SUPPER, Lucas said goodbye to his new young friend, then leaving the restaurant walked up to the front desk to rent a room.

"It's room 202," the clerk said in a cold, expressionless voice. "It's in the front, the first room on the right."

The clerk gave Lucas the key.

"Thanks," Lucas said, signing the hotel guest registration book.

"Check out time is eight o'clock."

"Eight o'clock? Isn't that a little early."

"It is our checkout time," the clerk repeated.

"Yeah, well it doesn't matter. I'll be gone before then, anyway." Lucas picked up his saddle bags and draped them over his right shoulder, then, holding his rifle in his left hand, climbed the stairs to the second floor. The stairway opened onto a long hallway. The hallway runner was maroon with a floral design. The wallpaper was of a cream color, well illuminated because there were gimbal-mounted kerosene lanterns flanking every door.

As the clerk had stated, room 202 was the first room on the right. At the end of the hallway, there was a window that looked out onto the street. Lucas extinguished the lantern nearest the window, so he could look out onto the street without being seen. Even though it was dark outside, there was enough light from the moon, and from the street lantern to see what was going on below. Across the street he saw two men sitting on the porch of the apothecary. They were smoking, and he could see the orange glow at the tip of the cigarettes. He also saw a soft gleam from a bottle they were sharing. Both men were wearing sombreros, so he knew they represented no danger to him.

Lucas unlocked the door to his room, stepped inside, then relocked the door. It was a typical hotel room with a bed, a washstand, a bedside table with a lantern, and a wooden chair. There were two windows which provided a welcome breeze.

Lucas took off his boots, laid the rifle and saddlebags on the floor beside the bed, hooked the pistol belt onto the bedstead so that he would have easy access to the pistol, then lay down. He was asleep within five minutes.

JUST NEXT DOOR to the hotel, Sam Coker was in the cantina, nursing his drink. The bartender told him that Cain was in town, right now. So, the question that faced Coker is what should he do about it? Should he take care of Cain before going back to see Stewart?

No, hell no! he thought. Look how many had tried already and failed. He knew that he would be no match for Lucas Cain. Still, he did have a significant advantage over Cain. He knew that Cain was in town, but Cain had no idea that he was. This almost seemed like too good an opportunity to pass up.

Coker was still pondering the question when someone approached his table. Looking up, he saw that it was an American.

"Mind if I share your table friend?" the American

asked. He pointed to the other cantina cliental. "I get a little tired at bein' surrounded by nothin' but a bunch of Mexes all the time."

"Yeah, I know what you mean," Coker said. He held up his glass. "This is tequila. Hell, a man can't even get a decent drink in here. I don't know how the hell an American could even live with all these Mexes."

"Are you kiddin'? When we play our cards right, Americans have it made here," the stranger said. He extended his hand. "The name is Gilmore, Frank Gilmore."

"Sam Coker."

"Coker? Yeah, I've seen your name on a dodger, haven't I? It's a pretty new one I think. But that's you, ain't it?

Coker's eyes narrowed. "That's not a very polite question to ask a man," he said. "It ain't a safe one to ask, neither."

Gilmore laughed. "That ain't nothin' for you to worry about. I ain't the law, 'n I sure as hell ain't no bounty hunter."

"Then why'd you even bring it up?"

"Because Lucas Cain is in town, right across the street, right now."

Coker raised his glass. "Yeah, that's what the bartender said. But just what makes you think I give a damn?"

"Oh, I know you're interested, Mr. Coker. You've been asking questions about your friend."

"Believe me Gilmore, he's no friend."

"He's on your trail, ain't he?"

"What business would that be of yours? Especially if you ain't the law or a bounty hunter like you said?"

"Coker, I think me 'n you could do a little business

together," Gilmore said. "That is, if you're game. You know that dodger I said that you was on? The reason I know about it, is 'cause I seen it down at the sheriff's office. You see, I'm the sheriff in this town."

"What?" Coker said sharply. "I thought you told me you wasn't the law."

Gilmore chuckled. "Don't get your dander up. I said that 'cause I sure ain't the kind of law you got to worry about. You see, I've sort of got me an arrangement worked out with this town, 'n it's one sweet deal. I been bleedin' these Mex's dry. They's payin' taxes for this, 'n taxes for that. 'N ever' time I can think up a new one, why, I hit 'em again."

"Wait a minute. Are you sayin' you put all these taxes on the town, 'n ever' one paid?"

"Oh, yeah, they paid. They grumbled about it, but there didn't never none of 'em get the idea that they didn't have to pay. Also, I've worked out a deal with outlaws that was on the run. They pay me, 'n they can drink in the cantina, eat a good meal in the restaurant, 'n visit with the whores without worryin' none about bein' arrested, even if their names was on a dodger."

"Sounds like you got yourselves a pretty good deal goin'," Coker said. "Is that why you come over to my table? To get me to pay so I can stay here?"

Gilmore chuckled again. "Yeah, I want you to pay me, but not the way you think."

"What are you talking about?"

"I want you to help me get rid of Cain. And I know it's somethin' you want, too, so I figure we can work together on it."

"Why do you think you need to get rid of 'im? If you know anything about him, he don't never stay in one place very long."

"I'm afraid that Cain bein' here, might give the people some backbone so as they won't want to be paying the taxes anymore. But if someone was to kill Cain, why that would take all the backbone out of the citizens of this town. If they was to see that even a man like Lucas Cain could get hisself kilt, they would think twice a' fore tryin' anythin' on their own."

"So, what are you sayin', Gilmore? Are you plannin' on killin' Cain? Because if you are, you need to know that Cain is someone that takes a heap of killin'."

"Yeah, but I figure if we go in together to get 'im killed, we'll be able to do it."

"What do you mean, together? I ain't got no investment in this town. You're the one who'll be the sheriff, not me."

"Yeah, that may be true. But unless I miss my guess, you want him kilt just as much as I do. And if you don't, you should. You're a wanted man, Coker, and believe me, if Cain wants to find you, he'll damn well do it."

"All right, let's say that I do want him dead. You got 'ny idea how to go about it? 'Cause me 'n some o' my friends been tryin' to kill this son of a bitch for some time now, only we ain't had no luck in gettin' it done. It's like I told you before, Cain takes a heap o' killin'."

"Yeah, well, it might be some easier iffen we was to kill 'im whilst he was a' sleepin' in bed."

"How we goin' to get to 'im, without the desk clerk givin' some kind of a alarm?"

Gilmore laughed out loud. "That's a good one," he said.

"What do you mean, it's a good one?"

"The desk clerk is my brother. If I can get control of this town, that's the same as my brother havin' control."

Coker reached across the table. "Gilmore, iffen it's

true that you really do want that son of a bitch dead, then you got yourself, a partner."

THE YOUNG MEXICAN boy who had taken care of Lucas's horse and shared supper with him, was mopping the saloon floor. When he heard the two men talking about killing Lucas, he mopped in the same place long enough to get the gist of the conversation, then while the two men were still at the table, he left the saloon and hurried down to the hotel.

The hotel desk clerk was reading the newspaper when the boy stepped up to the desk.

"*Señor?*"

"What do you want?" the desk clerk asked, gruffly.

"*Señor* Cain, he is here, in the hotel?"

"Yeah, what about it?"

"What room is he in?"

"Why do you need to know?"

"I put his horse in the livery for him. His horse needs a shoe, and *Señor* Curtis said I must tell him."

"He's in room 202."

"*Gracias.*"

LUCAS WAS BACK on the Shiloh battlefield. The sun was low, and the battlefield was red with its glow. Lucas had never seen such red. It blazed up at him with the deep crimson of blood. It was blood! The ground was covered with blood!

"*Señor!*"

The warning cry cut through the layers of sleep as quickly as a fly reacting to a hand swipe. The dream fell away, and Lucas, lay awake for a moment, wondering who had called out to him.

"*Señor*?" The call was repeated and now Lucas recognized the voice. It was the young Mexican boy.

Lucas rolled out of bed, then crossed the room to open the door. "Hello, *amigo*," he said, "what do you need?"

"*Señor*, the *alguacil* and a man named Coker are going to try and kill you tonight. I heard them talking."

"The sheriff wants to kill me?"

"*Si*, the *alguacil* is an evil man."

"Thanks for the warning," Lucas said. "Come on inside. If they see you here, they might get suspicious."

"*Si*," the young Mexican replied.

"Over there, in the corner," Lucas said. "That way, you'll be out of the line of fire, if shooting breaks out."

"*Si*," the boy said, moving quickly into the room.

Lucas looked up and down the hallway and seeing no one, he stepped back inside, closed, and locked the door.

22

Gilmore and Coker had one more drink before leaving the cantina. Both men loosened the pistols in their holsters, even though neither of them anticipated the necessity for a quick draw. They knew that if Cain was given the chance of a draw, he very well could beat both of them. No, their best bet would be to shoot Cain as he slept. And that is exactly what they planned to do.

"I'll find out which room is his and get a key to the door," Gilmore said.

"You can do that?"

"Yeah, it's like I told you, the desk clerk is my brother."

Coker waited at the foot of the stairs until Gilmore returned, smiling, and holding up the key.

"It's room 202," Gilmore said. "And I get the first shot. I need the town to know that I'm the one that killed him."

"Go ahead," Coker said. "I just want the son of a bitch dead and I don't care who does it."

With gun in hand, the two men crept up the stairs.

LUCAS HEARD the sound of a key being put into the lock of his door. The Mexican boy was sleeping on the floor and Lucas woke him up.

"*Señor?*" the boy asked.

"Shh,"" Lucas hissed. He pointed to the corner of the room and made a motion with his hand.

The boy realized then what Lucas was doing, and without a word, he hurried over to the corner.

After getting the boy in the safety of the corner, Lucas pulled his gun from the holster that hung from the headboard of his bed then knelt behind it, just as his, now-unlocked, door was opened. Lucas waited for a second, then a gun fired from the doorway. The bullet sent up a puff of feathers from the pillow, where Lucas' head would have been if he had not heard the sound of the key being thrust into the lock.

The shooter was temporarily blinded by the muzzle flash, and he remained in the door for a moment to make certain Lucas was dead. The advantage now belonged to Lucas. He aimed at the man who was standing in the doorway, and closing his eyes against the muzzle flash, pulled the trigger. The gun bucked in his hand, and the roar of the exploding cartridge filled the room.

To Lucas, there was a measurable moment of time between the shots, but to the others in the hotel and the occupants of the adjacent buildings, the two shots were so close together, that it sounded like the shots were simultaneous.

The citizens of the town were used to the discharges of pistols fired by saloon patrons in fits of drunken excess. But they knew, instinctively, that these were not shots fired in fun or celebration. These were serious shots, and someone had just died. Many of the citizens who were close enough to hear the shots crossed themselves in prayer for the victim.

Lucas heard a groan, then the sound of his target falling to the floor.

"WHAT THE HELL?" Coker said, quietly when he saw Gilmore go down. Turning, he ran down to the head of the stairs, went down a few steps, they lay back across them so he could see the door to the room, while he because of the stairs, was partially obscured. He aimed at the open door knowing that Cain would step out into the hallway.

"*SEÑOR? SEÑOR*, ARE YOU SHOT?" the young Mexican boy asked in a quiet, and frightened voice.

"No, I'm all right," Lucas said. Regaining his feet, he moved to the doorway and stepped over the body to look out into the hall. The boy left his corner and came to the doorway with Lucas.

"This is *Señor* Gilmore, the *alguacil*," the boy said. "He was one of the *hombres* I heard planning to kill you."

There was another gunshot then, and Lucas saw the muzzle flash a short distance down the hall at the head of the stairs. Lucas threw a bullet that way but he knew, even as he was shooting, that the target was gone. Lucas hurried to the top of the stairs, and saw the shooter running down them. He raised his pistol to shoot, but held fire when he saw two or three people at the foot of the stairs, drawn there by curiosity.

"*Señor*! *Señor*!" the Mexican boy called, and this time Lucas heard pain in the voice. He hurried back down to the door of his room, where he saw the boy sitting on the floor leaning against the wall.

"I am shot, *Señor*," the boy said. "It was the man who got away."

Lucas relit the lantern in his room, then carried it over to have a closer look at the boy. The light of the lantern disclosed that he had been shot in the stomach.

"I am sorry, *Señor*, I should have stayed in the room like you said." The pain was evident in the voice as the boy spoke.

By now two or three people had come up, made curious by the shooting.

"Is there a doctor in this town?" Lucas asked.

"Yeah, we have a very good doctor," one of the men replied.

"Go get him, the boy has been hurt."

"All right," the man answered.

Lucas carried the lantern over for a closer examination of the body of the man he shot.

"Will you be wantin' a doctor for Gilmore as well?" one of the remaining men asked, with a nod toward the man lying in the hallway, right in front of the door that opened into Lucas's room.

"He doesn't have any need for a doctor," Lucas said. "He's dead."

"Were there two of them?"

"Yes. According to the boy, the other man's name was Coker. I'm pretty sure that Coker is one of Stewart's men."

"You were lucky."

"I had help from the boy here," Lucas said with a nod toward the small figure who was sitting on the floor holding his hand over his stomach.

"I came to warn you, when I heard them talking," the boy said, his voice weaker now than it was before.

"And you saved my life," Lucas said.

"I am glad that I could. We are *amigos*, are we not?"

"Yes, we are *amigos*."

"Let me through, let me through," someone was calling from the head of the stairs. "I'm a doctor."

Those who had gathered at the scene parted, and the doctor hurried to the boy's side then knelt down to examine the wound. "I will need a bed for him."

"Use that one," Lucas said, pointing to his bed.

"You men, get him in bed," the doctor said.

As the two men picked up the boy, Lucas walked over to the window and looked outside. At the far end of the town, he saw a man riding out of town, fast, and he knew it had to be Coker.

"Mr. Cain?" the doctor said.

"Yes?"

"I thought you might want to know. The boy just died."

"Damn," Lucas said. He pinched the bridge of his nose and lowered his head. He had the same feeling about the boy dying, that he did about losing friends during the war. Damn, he didn't even know the boy's name.

"What was his name?" Lucas asked.

"The only name anyone knew him by was Juan," one of the men responded.

COKER HELD his horse at a gallop until he was well out of town, then he slowed to a swift walk. It was twenty miles to El Pueblo where he would meet the others, and he planned to be there by dawn. Stewart had sent him to find out what happened to Calhoun. Well, he found out. He also found out where Cain was, and he may or may not have killed him.

He was pretty sure he had killed him. He had the advantage; he was lying at the head of the stairs when he saw, or thought he saw, Cain step out from his room. It was dark with the only hall light being several rooms down from Cain's room, so all he saw was a shadow.

But, the shadow made a pretty good target, so Coker was reasonably satisfied that he hadn't missed.

He thought of what the reaction would be from the others, when they learned that he had killed Cain.

"What do you think, horse?" Coker asked. "Do you think I killed him?"

The horse gave a little whinny.

"Yeah," Coker said. "I think I did, too."

LUCAS, very much wanted to go after Coker, and if Juan had not died in his very bed, he would have done so. But the boy saved his life, and there was no way he was going to abandon him now. He stayed in La Cuesta, but because he didn't want to spend the rest of the night in the same bed where the boy died, he decided to sleep in the straw of the same stall Charley II occupied at the livery stable

---

COKER HAD BEEN PUSHING his horse pretty hard, and within an hour after riding out of La Cuesta, he felt his horse go lame. He knew he should probably dismount, but he needed to get as far away from La Cuesta as he possibly could. He might have hit Cain, or he might have actually hit the boy instead. All he knew was that he heard a grunt after he shot and he was pretty sure that it was a grunt of pain.

Either way, he needed to put as much distance between him and La Cuesta as he possible could, under the circumstances.

Back in La Cuesta, the undertaker had two bodies to deal with. Gilmore was the deputy sheriff, so his burial expenses would be paid by the county, even though he had very few actual supporters.

"What about the boy?" someone asked.

"He has no next of kin as far as anyone knows," Ponder, the undertaker said. "I'll put 'im in a box, and bury him in Potter's Field."

"You will not, sir," Lucas said. "You'll put Juan in your finest coffin, and you'll bury him in the best plot available."

"Who's going to pay for that?" Ponder asked.

"I will."

There were considerably more people at the cemetery for the burying of the two bodies than Lucas would have expected. There were several there for the burial of Thaddeus J. Gilmore, because Gilmore was the sheriff. Many of those who came did so out of a degree of curiosity, and just as many came because, in the words of one of the town's people, he just wanted "to start the son of a bitch on his way to hell."

THERE WERE ALSO a number of people there to send Juan off. Many knew who Juan was, but few actually knew him. Nobody knew his age, though most supposed him to be somewhere between twelve and fourteen. He had no family that anyone knew of. He might have been raised in an orphanage, but nobody knew for sure, because he just showed up in the town about a year earlier. Also, he was without a last name. Or at least, everyone thought he had no last name. They were very surprised when they saw the inscription on his tombstone.

Juan Cain
A young man of
Courage and Dignity
May he rest in peace

23

Juan had identified the two men who had plotted to kill Lucas as Coker and Gilmore. He knew Sam Coker to be one of Stewart's men. After the burial, Lucas left town, going in the direction he had seen the rider leaving the night before. It was mid-morning, and the sun showed that it was halfway to noon. Ahead of him, the sunburned land lay in empty folds of rocks, hot, yellow sand, and prickly cactus. Undulating waves rose up from the sun-heated ground, causing those objects close by to shimmer and form ghost lakes to lie tantalizingly in the distance.

The horse of the rider Lucas was trailing went lame. Lucas picked it up immediately by the animal's gait and the slight dragging of one foot. He also knew that it wasn't something simple, like a loose shoe, or even a stone bruise. This was serious, and Lucas was certain that Coker was going to have to dismount. About a mile further, Lucas's belief that the rider would have to dismount was borne out, when later, he saw footprints appear on the trail.

The question now, was when did this happen? Lucas had seen the rider leave around midnight, and because it was nearly noon, that was coming up on a twelve-hour head-start.

It had still been dark when Coker shot his horse. He walked for about another hour until he could walk no more, then he lay down behind some rocks so he couldn't be seen from the road, and fell into an exhausted sleep. He woke up just after dawn, then began walking again. He had no idea how far he was from El Pueblo, but he hoped he would get there before Stewart and the others left to rob the bank. He didn't want to be left out.

About mid-morning he saw a buckboard coming toward him, and he stood to one side of the road and waited. As it drew closer, he saw that there was a man driving with a woman by his side. They stopped when they reached him.

"Mister, you're a long way away from anywhere to be on foot," the man said in a friendly tone of voice.

"Yeah, I had to put my horse down last night."

"Well, we're headed into town. If you'd like, you can climb aboard and we'll get you there."

"Yeah, thanks," Coker said, though he had absolutely no intention of returning to the town he had just left.

"Let me get this back seat up for you," the man said. Climbing down from the buckboard, he elevated the back seat, then turned toward Coker with a welcoming smile.

"Here you go, it's all ready for you," the man said. The expression on his face turned from a friendly smile to one of fear when he saw that Coker was pointing a gun at him.

"Here, what is this? I told you we'd help you get to La Cuesta," the man said.

"Yeah, well, the thing is, I don't want to go to La Cuesta," Coker replied in a cold tone of voice.

Coker pulled the trigger.

WHEN LUCAS REACHED the horse Coker had put down, he saw that the saddle hadn't been removed. Coker was now afoot, and that greatly increased the chances of him being found. He followed the boot prints to the southwest. Figuring a horse could cover ground twice as fast as a man on foot, Lucas calculated that he would catch up with Coker by early afternoon.

Lucas was riding alongside a low ridge when he heard the shot. The shot was followed by a woman's scream, then there was another shot. Lucas kicked his horse into a gallop and within a few moments, crested a hill. There, on the road below him, he saw a buckboard standing unattached in the middle of the road. As he drew even closer, he saw a man and a woman. The man lay on the road, the woman was sitting on the road beside him, holding his head in her lap and she was crying.

As Lucas drew closer, the woman looked up toward him, then began screaming again.

"Easy, ma'am, easy," Lucas said, speaking as comfortingly as he could. "I'm here to help you, not to hurt you. What happened here?"

"It's my husband. He's been shot. Help him, please help him."

Lucas dismounted, then squatted down beside the body as he spoke. "Who shot him?"

"It was a man," the woman said. "He didn't have a horse, so Elmer, my husband, said that he thought we should stop and help him. When we did, the man shot him."

As she was speaking, Lucas was examining the body.

"Is he...is he dead?" the woman asked in a pained voice.

"Yes, ma'am, I'm afraid he is," Lucas answered.

The woman began sobbing, and all Lucas could do was stand there, silently. He didn't know what to say to her to ease her pain. That was when he noticed blood on her dress.

"Ma'am? Were you shot as well?"

"I don't know," the woman answered. She looked down at herself, then looked at her leg. "Yes," she said, hesitantly. "Yes, I suppose I was shot, in the leg. That's funny, I don't remember being shot. I just...I just..." The woman's eyelids began to flutter, then they closed, and she fell back in a dead faint.

"Damn," Lucas said quietly. He had to hand it to Coker. It was an act of genius, evil genius to be sure, but genius, nevertheless. He had killed the man, and wounded the woman. If he had killed both of them, Lucas could have stayed on his trail, but by leaving the woman alive and wounded, he had given Lucas no choice but to look after the woman and that would mean taking her back to where she and her husband lived.

"Sorry, Charley," Lucas said as he removed the saddle. "I'm afraid you're going to have to pull this buckboard. I know pulling a buckboard is beneath you, but it can't be helped."

MRS. BIZZELL TOLD Lucas that she lived on a small farm some four miles back. She was unable to direct him though, because she spent most of the trip lying in the back of the buckboard, drifting in and out of consciousness. Lucas found the ranch by following the buckboard wheel tracks back the way they came. Charley II was uncomfortable in the buckboard traces, and he fought and fidgeted all the way. It was an uncomfortable trip, but he finally pulled up in front of small farm house.

"Is this it, Mrs. Bizzell?" Lucas asked.

The woman had been sleeping for most of the way, so she opened her eyes and looked at the rather small house with a sense of belonging.

"Yes, this is our house."

Lucas carried her into the house, and laid her on her bed. He saw, as if seeing her for the first time, that she was actually quite pretty, even though her face was contorted with pain.

The shock and pain of being moved around kept Mrs. Bizzell unconscious for most of the time, and for that, Lucas was glad. Now he was going to have to find the wound.

Lucas cut the bottom half of her dress off, then the petticoat, and finally the leg of her bloomers. In order to get to the wound, he had to cut her bloomers quite high, though he managed to leave enough cloth to preserve a modicum of modesty. He didn't want her to wake up and think there was something untoward going on. The entry wound of the bullet was in her left thigh, about eight inches above the knee. The blood was dark and ugly, but Lucas didn't see any signs of gangrene, so he was pretty sure he would be able to extract the bullet, if she would let him.

He got some water and a cloth and began bathing her face until she woke up.

The woman looked at him for a moment as if trying to figure out where she was, and who he was. Then she remembered and she raised her hand to her mouth.

"My husband?"

"I'm sorry, ma'am."

"Elmer's dead, isn't he?"

"Yes, ma'am."

"Where is he? Oh, you didn't leave him out in the middle of the road, did you?"

"No, ma'am, he came back with us. He's out in the buckboard."

"Have I been shot?"

"Yes, ma'am, you have."

"Am I...am I dying?"

"No, ma'am, you aren't dying, but I'm going to have to take the bullet out, if you will let me."

"Of course, I'll let you. Why wouldn't I?"

"Well, there are a couple of reasons," Lucas replied. "For one thing, it's going to hurt."

"I have a high tolerance for pain. I've given birth."

"Oh," Lucas said, looking around in surprise. "Is there a child?"

"There was. A little girl. She died last winter."

"Oh, I'm so sorry to hear that."

"You said there were a couple of reasons?"

"Yes, for another thing, it's in a rather delicate spot. It's in your left leg, pretty high above the knee."

The woman put her hand down to feel her leg. It wasn't until then that she realized her leg was bare. She looked up at Lucas with questioning eyes.

"I'm sorry," Lucas said. "I had to find the bullet."

"Yes." Mrs. Bizzell sighed. "Well, you've found it, so how much more delicate can it be?"

"I'll need to get a fire started," Lucas said.

"There's wood in the box and matches above the stove."

"Thanks, I'll get the fire going." Lucas saw a bottle of whiskey. "Oh, and Mrs. Bizzell, I don't want to offend you, but it might help some with the pain of my digging around for the bullet if you could drink some whiskey."

The woman laughed. "Now, tell me, Lucas Cain, just why you think I would be offended by drinking a little whiskey. I used to drink whiskey for a living. Well, most of the time it was tea, but sometimes it was whiskey. Especially if I wanted something to take my mind off how ugly, or crude, or just mean, the man was. Bring me the bottle."

Lucas looked at her in surprise. "Mrs. Bizzell, do you know me?"

"Yes, I know you. And you know me as well. The only thing is, you knew me as Cindy."

"Wait a minute. Are you Naomi Ragland?" Lucas asked.

"Yes, how did you..." Naomi started, then she stopped, and despite the pain, smiled. "I told you my real name when you took me out to the Rustic Rock, didn't I?"

"Yes, you did."

"I'm flattered that you remember."

"I'm sorry I didn't recognize you."

"That's all right, there's no reason you should have. I don't look anything at all now like I did then, when I wore different dresses and a lot of makeup. Besides, we're a long way from The Mud Slide Saloon and Topeka."

Lucas handed her the bottle and a glass, but she gave the glass back, then pulled the cork and drank right from the bottle.

"You do look different," Lucas said. "Just as pretty, but different."

"I suppose I do," Naomi said after she took the first swallow. "I was Cindy at The Mud Slide for three years. Then, two years ago, Elmer Bizzell asked me if he could take me away from all that. The other girls thought I was crazy to give up the sporting life to become a farmer's wife."

Naomi was quiet for a moment, and Lucas saw the tears sliding down her cheeks.

"Elmer was a good man and a good husband," she said. "And I never regretted it for a minute. Not for one minute."

"If you went with him, then there is no doubt in my mind, but that he was a good man."

Naomi wept quietly for a few moments, and Lucas allowed her some time to deal with her grief.

Naomi wiped her tears away, then reached out to lay her hand on Lucas's arm. "You were a good man, too, Lucas. All the other girls at The Mud Slide commented on how quiet you always were. Quiet and polite. There were so few of the men we drank with, who were quiet."

"It doesn't cost anything to be polite," Lucas said. He nodded toward the bottle. "How much of that can you drink? Can you drink enough for it to ease the pain?"

Naomi smiled at him. "I may have given up the sporting life, Lucas, but I haven't lost my taste for liquor. How about if I just finish off the whole bottle?"

"Yes, that would be good, and that would probably do it."

Lucas got the fire started in the stove while Naomi finished the whole bottle. Then, when she was good and drunk and the stove was roaring hot, he heated up his knife and walked over to look down at her.

"Are you ready?"

Naomi nodded. "I'm as ready as I'll ever be."

Lucas gave her a rolled-up cloth. "Here you go, Naomi, bite down on this."

Naomi took the cloth, nodded at Lucas, then closed her eyes.

24

After he had extracted the bullet, then seared the bullet hole closed, Naomi lay on her bed. She was passed out, either from the pain, or from the whiskey, he didn't know which, but he was glad that she was.

As he stood there looking down at her sleeping form, he recalled the incident in the Rustic Rock that Naomi had spoken of.

"Caleb?" Lucas called.

The bartender moved down to see what Lucas wanted.

"How much money does Cindy make for the saloon in one night?"

"Why do you ask?"

"How much?" Lucas repeated without answering Caleb's question.

"About ten dollars."

Lucas took a twenty-dollar bill from his wallet, and handed it to Caleb.

"Why did you do that?" Cindy asked, surprised and confused by Lucas's action.

Lucas gave Cindy a twenty-dollar bill. "I want you to change clothes, then come away from the saloon with me for tonight."

"Oh, Deputy Cain, it doesn't cost you that much."

"I don't want to do 'it,'" Lucas said, with emphasis on the word it. "I want your company, that's all. Now, change from this..." Lucas made a motion with his hand to take in the revealing clothes Cindy was wearing, "into something you can wear in the restaurant."

Cindy smiled. "I'll be right back down."

When Cindy came back downstairs, she was wearing a dress that she could wear to church.

"You look very nice," Lucas said.

"Thank you," Cindy replied.

Lucas believed that he actually saw Cindy blush.

Lucas took her to the Rustic Rock, which was Cindy's first time, ever, to be in the nicest restaurant in town.

"They won't like for me to be in here," Cindy said.

"That's all right," Lucas said. "They'll like my money."

Cindy chuckled. "I suppose they will."

They were seated without any difficulty, but once they were at the table, Cindy whispered something to Lucas.

"There are three men in here who are glaring at me. They know who I am."

"Don't worry about it. If they give you any trouble, they'll answer to me."

Cindy chuckled. "I don't think they'll give me any trouble. All three of them are here with their wives."

"You want to go say hello to them?"

"What? No, I—" Cindy paused in mid-sentence when she saw that Lucas was grinning. "On the other hand, maybe I should," she said, laughing, and bringing laughter from Lucas.

"What's your name?" Lucas asked, over the steaks they were eating.

"Why, you know my name," Cindy said, surprised by the question.

"No, Cindy is the name you're using. What I want to know is, what's your real name."

"I never tell my real—" She paused for a second, then smiled at him. "It's Naomi Ragland."

"That's a pretty name, so for this meal, I'll call you Naomi."

Lucas saw tears come to Naomi's eyes.

"I'm sorry," Lucas said. "Would you rather me not call you Naomi?"

"No, I..." Naomi wiped her eyes. "I'm sorry. It's just that, well, it feels good to have someone call me by my right name."

LUCAS TOOK a pan of biscuits from the oven, then he checked on the bacon. In another pan he was frying potatoes, and as soon as the bacon came out, he stirred in flour to make gravy. Behind him, he heard Naomi groan. He set the skillet aside to keep from burning anything, then walked over to her bed to check on her.

"Good morning," Lucas said.

"Oh, don't shout at me," Naomi said, putting her hands to her head.

Lucas chuckled. "All right, I'll be quiet," he said, speaking just above a whisper.

"I slept through the whole night?" She asked.

"You were in and out, mostly out. How do you feel?"

"My leg hurts."

"I'm sure it does, but it isn't festering, and that's a good sign," Lucas said. "How's your head?"

"My head?" Again, she put her hands to her head. "Yes, now that you ask, it does hurt."

"I shouldn't wonder. You put away an entire bottle of whiskey last night."

"A hangover? My God, I do have a hangover, don't I? I haven't had a hangover in two years."

"It was worth it. It kept you knocked out, so I was able to work on your leg."

Naomi sniffed a couple of times. "My, something smells good."

"That's a good sign," Lucas said. "If you're hungry, even with a hangover, I would say that your leg is just fine."

"Yes, I am hungry." She sat up and swung her legs over the edge of the bed, then looked at the bandage. "You did a pretty good job with this," she said.

"Well, I've patched a few bullet and knife wounds in my day," Lucas replied.

"I guess you have. Lucas, I'd like to eat at the table, if I can."

"Sure, I don't see why not," Lucas agreed. He helped her up, but she was able to walk to the table by herself.

"What did you do with Elmer?" Naomi asked.

"I found Minnie's grave. I took it that she was you daughter, so I buried Elmer right beside her so he could keep an eye on her."

Naomi was quiet, and though her eyes glistened with tears, she didn't cry aloud.

Lucas helped her sit down, then he brought food over from the cook stove, and they began to eat.

"The man who shot Elmer and stole our horse was running from you, wasn't he?"

"Yes."

"What's his name?"

"Sam Coker."

"What's he wanted for?"

"He's a member of Dudley Stewart's gang, and that means he's guilty of murder and robbery. I was after him, hoping he would lead me to Stewart."

"Well, now you've got another reason to be looking for him," Naomi said.

"Indeed, I do. I will be hunting him down for the murder of Elmer Bizzell."

Naomi chewed thoughtfully, and was quiet for a moment. Then she spoke. "Not if you hang around here any longer."

"Yes, I was going to talk to you about that," Lucas said. "Do you think you will be all right here, by yourself?"

"Yes, I know I will. I want you to go after that, and excuse my language here, but I want you to go after that son of a bitch. And when you find him, I want you to shoot him dead. And while you're doing that, take a moment to think about Elmer."

"And Juan," Lucas said.

"Who's Juan?"

Lucas told her about the young Mexican boy who had saved his life.

"And yes, think of Juan as well," Naomi said.

Coker had camped out for the night, taking the opportunity to get some rest because he knew that whoever was chasing him would have to take care of the woman he had shot. After the sun came up, he resumed his travel, but the horse he had taken yesterday wasn't being very cooperative.

"You miserable son of a bitch!" Coker said, hitting the horse with a length of trace line When Coker took the horse, it had been attached to a buckboard, and having left his saddle behind when he had put his horse down, he was now riding bare back. To add to his problems, the halter and harness were not designed for a rider. Also, the horse was not used to being ridden, and though he didn't buck Coker off, he was balky and hard to handle.

Sometimes the horse would just stop and refuse to move, and no amount of urging would get him going again. When that would happen, Coker had no choice but to get off the horse, grab the trace line, and start walking, pulling the horse behind him. That would continue for several minutes, then he would climb up on the horse's back and start urging him to move again, with the same results as before.

Over the next two hours, Coker, by riding some of the time and walking the rest of the time, barely covered five miles.

"Let's go," he said, kicking his feet against the horse's sides. The kicking was without effect, because he wasn't wearing spurs.

"All right, all right!" he shouted at the balking horse, before dismounting yet again, and walking around to the front of the horse.

"I tell you what I should 'a done. I should 'a just left you hooked up to the wagon. If I'd a' done that, I'd 'a been a hell of a lot farther along than I am now. No. No, what I should have done is kill that bastard, Cain."

After several more minutes, Coker was able to mount the horse again. Then, a few minutes after he had remounted, he heard the unmistakable and very welcome sound of a train whistle.

"A train whistle!" he said. "Son of a bitch, there's a train up ahead!"

Coker began kicking his legs against the side of the horse, trying to get it to break into a gallop. All he got for his efforts was a slight increase in the speed of the horse's walking. When he crested a ridge, he saw the train stopped at a water tower. The train was headed southeast. That was the wrong direction—he needed to be going northwest. He thought about it for a moment, then decided it didn't make any difference what direction the train was going. The only thing that was important was that he would get away from Lucas Cain. And the train would certainly allow him to do that.

"Hurry up, horse," he demanded, kicking the animal in its sides as hard as he could. "If you don't get me to the train on time, I'll sure as hell, blow your head off."

25

By the time Lucas reached the railroad tracks, the train had already left. There was no doubt in his mind, but that Coker had hopped aboard a train, because he found Naomi's horse tied to one of the legs of the water tower. A pencil-thin line of smoke on the distant horizon marked where the train was.

Lucas turned Naomi's horse loose, and was pleased to see that it trotted off in the right direction. Then he gave Charley II water, then took off his bedroll, long gun, and saddlebags, making the load as light as possible. There was still a chance he could catch the train if he was lucky. Of course, he wouldn't be able to catch the train by chasing after it, but there had to be a way.

Lucas knew that just to the east there were several deep ravines and spine-back ridges. The railroad had considered, in their wisdom, to route the tracks around such difficult terrain, rather than build bridges and trestles. As a result, the track bowed south, using a wide loop of track that covered ten miles, to advance but one mile.

The ridges and ravines weren't easy for a horse to

traverse either, but it could be done by a good and serious rider. Lucas figured that if he could cross to the other side, he would be able to meet the train.

Hiding his jettisoned equipment, Lucas tightened the saddle cinch, then mounted Charley II and pushed him into a ground-eating lope, reaching the badlands in just a few minutes. Traversing the ravines and ridges was much more difficult, and Lucas began to worry that perhaps he wouldn't be on the other side in time to catch the train. In fact, he would be lucky if he could reach the ridge, because there were many times when he would have to dismount, and lead his horse. It was hot, exhausting work, climbing up out of one gulley, only to find another one no more than a hundred yards ahead of him. But Lucas pressed on.

When he reached the far side of the gullies, he realized that he wasn't going to make it through in time. He let out a curse in frustration, then he saw something that might mean success after all.

As the train came out of the oxbow, it would have to pass through a long narrow and twisting gulley, between two high buttes. Lucas was just on the opposite side of one of those buttes now. If he could climb it quickly enough, he could, perhaps, get to the track before the train arrived. There was no way Charley II could make that climb, and he wasn't sure he could, but he was damn well going to try.

ON BOARD the train at that very moment, Coker was sitting at a window seat looking at the brown and yellow countryside as it passed by outside. A little wisp of smoke drifted by the window, and Coker looked ahead to see that the train was going around a curve, thus allowing him to see the engine. The driver wheels were pounding against the track, partly obscured by the white puffs of steam that feathered out from the drive cylinder.

Coker had no idea how fast they were going, but he was sure it was faster than a galloping horse.

The conductor passed down the aisle then, moving importantly from one part of the train to another.

"Conductor?"

The conductor responded to Coker's call.

"How fast would you say we're a' goin' right now?"

The conductor took out his watch, opened it, and stared at it for a few seconds, then he snapped it shut. "Right now we are doing just over twenty miles per hour."

"Twenty miles an hour? Can a horse run twenty miles an hour?"

"Well, a race horse can go a mile in two minutes, and that's thirty miles an hour. But only the fastest race horses can do that, and then only for a short time. This train can run at twenty miles an hour for an unlimited time bound only by its need for fuel and water," he added with a proud smile. "Don't forget, it is now possible for a person to travel all the way across the country, from the Atlantic to the Pacific Ocean in but a week. Time was, when such a trip would take six months. We live in a wondrous time, my friend. Yes, sir, a wondrous time indeed."

After the conductor left, Coker looked out through the window, frustrated because he couldn't see behind him. It worried him that the conductor said that a horse could run that fast, even for just a short time.

Coker leaned back in his seat.

Wait a minute, he thought. Now, suppose Cain was

riding a horse that could run as fast as this train. He would have to run even faster to catch up with the train, and because he had a good lead on him, the horse would have to run as fast as a race horse for the entire time.

Leaning back in the seat, he smiled. There was no way Cain was going to catch up with him. Then he remembered how many times Cain seemed to defy logic, and his sense of well-being faded. He leaned toward the window again, trying to look behind the train. He didn't see anything, but if he had seen a horse, doggedly racing after them, he wouldn't have been surprised.

LUCAS FOUND A SHADED GRASSY AREA, and decided he would leave his horse here. This was not any normal route of transit, so it was highly unlikely that anyone would discover Charley II here. He took off the saddle so that Charley II would be comfortable, then he started climbing.

Lucas was about to decide that he may have bitten off more than he could chew, because it was a much harder climb than he had anticipated. He had been climbing for half-an-hour, and could still see Charley II on the ground below him.

Lucas was now clinging to the wall of the cliff, moving only when he found the smallest crevice for his foot. Behind him was nothing but thin air, and if he missed a handhold or foothold, he would drop over a hundred feet to the rocks below.

Sweat was pouring into his eyes, but he couldn't let go, even to wipe his face. He thought he had about reached an impasse, and he was wondering if it wouldn't be better to turn around and go back. He had climbed more than half way up, but for the last few minutes, he had been unable to go any higher, because he couldn't find any footholds.

It was only with reluctance that he started back down. He would have to let Coker get away, while he went after the others. It wasn't what he wanted to do. Although Dudley Stewart was still his primary target, he had a special desire to get Coker now because Coker had killed Juan, but there was nothing he could do about it. If he went on, he could fall to his death on the rocks far below, and that wouldn't accomplish anything.

Lucas reached for the handhold he had surrendered a few moments earlier, taking the first step going back down. He got a good grip on the hold, then moved his foot into the step he had just left. But this time the slate that had held his weight on the way up failed to support him, and with a sickening sensation, he felt himself falling.

Lucas threw himself against the wall of the cliff as it scraped and tore at his body on the way down. Then, after a drop of some fifteen feet, he was able to break his fall by grabbing hold of a sturdy juniper tree. The tree supported his weight, and he hung there for a short while as he looked down at the gulley floor. He saw the slate that had broken free under his weight as it hit the bottom and shattered into pieces, far below.

Lucas looked to his right. There was a ledge about four feet away. It was a solid ledge, and if he could gain it, he would be all right. Taking a deep breath, he swung his feet to the right and up, grabbing the ledge with the heel of his boot. Gradually, he worked his feet up on to the ledge, and now he was bridged between the tree and the ledge.

He began pushing away from the juniper tree until

first one knee, then the other found a crevice. Finally, he felt secure enough to let go of the tree and work his way across until he was on the ledge.

After that it got easy. The ledge showed signs of having been a trail at one time, possibly an Indian trail that had existed until erosion took part of it away. After a few feet of inching his way across on his knees, he discovered that he could stand up and walk. A few feet farther, and he could walk as easily as if on the boardwalk in town. Somewhat later, he saw the railroad tracks, and in the distance, the approaching train. Smiling at his good fortune, he walked out to the edge and waited. Then, as the train passed underneath, he dropped down onto the mail car, which was the first car behind the tender. He squatted quickly to maintain his balance.

Although the train hadn't looked as if it were going so fast from above, now that he was on top of it, the ground seemed to be whipping past with blinding speed. There also was a pendulum effect with the sway of the train, with the wheels being the attaching point, and the top of the car being the outer end of the pendulum arm. That meant that from his position, the swaying of the car was so pronounced that it was difficult just to keep from falling off.

Lucas stayed on his hands and knees for a moment until he was sure he had his balance, then he took a deep breath, stood up, and started walking toward the rear of the train.

"MAMA! There's someone on top of the train!" a little girl said. She was in the same car Coker was in. Coker was in the first car behind the tender.

"Hush, dear," the little girl's mother said.

"But I saw him! I saw his shadow. He was walking toward the back of the train on top of the car. He was bent over."

"We'll ask the conductor," the little girl's mother suggested, and when the conductor passed through the car she summoned him.

"On top of the car?" the conductor replied to her question. "Oh, I wouldn't think so."

"But I saw his shadow on the ground," the little girl insisted.

The conductor moved over to the window. "Look," he said, "there's a man, there's another man, and that one looks like a bear, don't you think?"

"What is it?" the little girl's mother asked.

"It's the shadows," the conductor explained. "You see, as we pass through these cuts, there are many rocks of strange formations, and they cast their shadows upon the ground. Those shadows, combined with the speed at which we are moving, sometimes gives the most startling illusions. I once had a passenger insist that there was horse on the roof of the train. A horse, mind you," he said with a little chuckle.

"Oh," the little girl's mother said, "how foolish you must think we are."

"Not at all, madam," the conductor replied with a polite touch of his finger to the bill of his cap. "As I say, it happens all the time. Please, don't feel in the least embarrassed by it."

"Mama, it wasn't just a shadow it was a man, it really was," the little girl said after the conductor left.

"Hush, dear, you've caused enough of a scene as it is," her mother scolded gently.

COKER HAD OVERHEARD the entire conversation, and it was all he could do to hold down the bile of fear that had risen in his throat. He believed the little girl. Not only that, if the conductor had asked him, he could have given the shadow a name. He was just as certain of that as he was of his own name. He had no idea how he had managed to get on the roof of the train, but he knew that it was Lucas Cain.

Well, he wasn't going to stay inside just sitting here. No, sir. He was going to go after Cain.

Coker got up and walked to the front of the car, then out onto the platform. Looking up, he took a deep breath, then climbed to the top of the car. About two cars behind him, he saw a man running along the top of the car. It was Cain!

Because he was behind him, Coker realized that Cain had no idea that he was there. Coker climbed over the elevated channel on top of the car, then lay down behind it so he would have some shielding between himself and Cain. From this position, Coker used the elevated channel as a brace for his pistol, took careful aim, and fired.

Lucas heard the pop of the bullet passing so close to him, that he could feel the wind of its passing. He dropped down onto the top of the car in order to reduce his target profile. He fired back, missing Coker, but seeing his bullet send out a shower of sparks as it hit the boiler-plate steel that made up the back end of the tender.

Coker fired again, missing again. Then Lucas returned fire with three fast shots. Coker was sprayed with sparks from the bullets striking the elevated roof channel, but missing him because of the cover provided by the channel.

Because of the noise of the train, none of the passengers were aware of the drama being played out on top of the car. As the train went around a curve, it exposed Coker's position behind the roof channel. Lucas aimed carefully, then pulled the trigger. The result of the trigger pull was a click, as there was a dead round in the cylinder. He pulled the trigger a second time, and again, it was a misfire. He had only two bullets left, and both of them were duds.

Coker saw the two misfires, then realizing that he must be out of ammunition, stood up and ran down the length of the car, with his pistol extended before him. He reached Lucas, just as he had the opportunity to re-load.

"I've been waitin' a long time for this," Coker said. "You are one hard son of a bitch to kill, but I've got you now!"

Coker aimed his pistol at Lucas, but because his back was to the front of the train, he didn't see that they were headed for a small, hard-rock tunnel that marked the exit of the long, narrow draw.

"Say your prayers, Cain."

The train was almost to the tunnel opening.

"Look out behind you," Lucas shouted.

Coker's face took on an evil smile. "You think I'm going to...uh!"

Coker's head, traveling at twenty miles per hour, slammed hard into the rocky arch of the tunnel. Lucas saw a misty spray of blood from Coker's head, then he was gone over the side of the train. Lucas pressed himself down flat on the top of the car as the low tunnel passed over his head. When they were on the other side, he stood up and hurried to the rear of the train, then he climbed down and dropped off onto the track. He ran back down the track and through the tunnel to look for Coker. He found him lying grotesquely twisted alongside the track, with his neck and back broken. He was dead.

Lucas went through Coker's pockets and found seventy-two dollars in cash. Then he moved the body off to the side of the track, and buried it under a pile of rocks. Later, he would come back and retrieve the body to prove his claim for the reward. But for now, Coker would have to stay put.

There was also a piece of paper in Coker's pocket. On the paper were written two words.

Pecos. Thursday

It took Lucas three hours to get back to where he had left Charley II hobbled. There had been enough grass to keep him busy, and he didn't appear to be in any stress when Lucas returned to him.

"Good boy," Lucas said, stroking his horse on his nose. "I'm sorry I had to leave you like this, but where I was going, you couldn't go. But I'll need you for the next part of the trip. We're going to a town called Pecos. We can both get a drink there. Water for you, and beer for me."

26

Stewart, Bundy, and Owens were at the Horseshoe Saloon in El Pueblo. Bundy was at one of the tables, making an arrangement with one of the bar girls to go upstairs with him. Stewart was at the bar; Owens was sitting at a table in the back of the saloon.

Stewart came back to the table carrying a full bottle and two empty glasses. "Bundy doesn't want to drink with us?" he asked.

Owens looked over at the table where Bundy and the bar girl were negotiating, then laughed, low and deep in his throat. "Bundy's got other things on his mind," he said.

Stewart poured the whiskey into the two glasses, then pushed one of them across the table to Owens.

"See that fella down at the end of the bar?" Stewart said.

Owens turned to look in the direction Stewart had indicated.

"What about 'im?" Owens asked.

"He's a cattle buyer. He'll be takin' the stage into Pecos tomorrow lookin' to buy a whole herd."

"That takes a lot of money, don't it?" Owens asked.

"Yeah, it does."

"Hey, why don't we—?" Owens started to say, but Stewart cut him off.

"I know what you're about to ask and the answer is, he won't have it with him."

"Well, damn, where is it?"

"I heard him talkin' to another man. Turns out, all his money is in the bank in Pecos. Looks like there's going to be a lot more money than we thought. Maybe even twice as much."

"Dayum!" Owens said. "Feller gets money like that, he'll be rich as all get-out."

"Rich enough," Stewart replied

"When you figure Coker and Calhoun will get here?" Owens asked.

"Well, I'm not sure they *will* be here."

"You think Cain got 'em do you?"

"I'd be willin' to bet on it."

"Well, then I don't figure we'll be a' sharin' none o' the money with 'im then, will we?"

"Nope. 'N we won't be sharin' none with Bundy, neither," Stewart said.

"How we goin' to do that?"

Stewart nodded toward Bundy. "We was plannin' on goin' to Pecos tomorrow, weren't we?"

"Yes."

"We'll go today."

"Today?"

"Yes, today. Unless I miss my guess, Bundy 'n that whore will be upstairs in a little while. When they do go up, we'll ride over to Pecos, take care of our business 'n be gone before Bundy even knows we ain't here no more."

"Damn, Stewart, iffen we do that, Bundy's goin' to be some pissed off at us."

"So?"

"He's liable to come gunnin' for us."

"What difference does that make? Cain's already comin' for us, ain't he?"

"Yeah, I guess maybe you're right."

"I figure on gettin' out of here soon as we pull the job," Stewart said.

"Where will you be a' goin'?" Owens asked.

"I'm not sure, but I'm thinkin' about Denver, maybe, or Kansas City, or maybe even San Francisco."

"I'll be goin' to St. Louis," Owens said. He chuckled. "I seen me a picture of a real purty woman on a calendar oncest, 'n she was holdin' up a bottle of beer. It said on the calendar, "St. Louis's finest," so I figure she must be from St. Louis. I b'lieve that is the best lookin' woman I've ever seen, 'n I plan to go to St. Louis 'n find 'er."

"What makes you think a woman like that would have anything to do with someone like you?" Stewart asked.

"On account of I'll have a lot of money," Owens replied with a wide grin. "Anyhow, if I don't find her, I'll at least find the beer."

"Hey, Stewart!" Bundy called over from the table where he and the bargirl were standing. "Me 'n Aggie's goin' upstairs. I'll see you fellas tomorra for breakfast."

"Be ready to ride," Stewart replied.

"I will be, don't you worry none about that."

Stewart and Owens watched Bundy climb the stairs with Aggie.

"Stewart, do you think we'll be able to pull this off

with just the two of us?" Owens asked. "That's a lot fewer of us than we started with."

"Yeah, nothin' to it," Stewart said. "Look, here's the bank, here's the hotel, 'n here's the depot," Stewart said, putting his finger at different places on the table. "We'll tie the horses up out back, that way, nobody'll notice nothin'. We'll go in through the front door, take the money, 'n leave through the back door. Hell, it'll be easy as pie."

"Except for Cain," Owens pointed out.

"Damnit, Owens, will you get off my back about Cain?" Stewart demanded. "Didn't I tell you that he won't be no problem? By the time he finds out that we've robbed a bank in Pecos we'll be long gone to San Francisco or St. Louis, or wherever."

"Yeah," Owens said. "If we get the money. What I'm afraid is, Cain might show up in time to keep us from even doin' that."

"Damn, Owens, listen to you," Stewart said. "Here's the thing you need to remember. Cain ain't no ghost, he's a human bein'. Have you got that? He's a human bein', 'n he's just like all other human bein's, there ain't no difference at all."

"But he's different," Owens insisted. "Anyone else would be dead by now."

"Are you changin' your mind?" Stewart asked. "Maybe we ought not to rob the bank in Pecos. Maybe we should just go to the sheriff's office 'n turn ourselves in."

"I ain't changin' my mind about nothin'," Owens said. "All I'm a' sayin' is, we'll be makin' us one hell of a big mistake iffin we don't keep Lucas Cain in mind."

"We'll think about 'im later," Stewart said, standing

up. “Come on, we need to be gettin’ on our way now if we’re goin’ to get over to Pecos before the bank closes.”

“You mean we really are a’ goin’ to leave Bundy behind?” Owens asked.

“You want to stay behind ‘n wait on ‘im, well you just go right on ahead ‘n do it,” Stewart said. “Onliest thing is, we’ve got to get over to Pecos before the bank closes. Now, are you a’ comin’, or ain’t ya?”

“I’m comin’, I’m comin’,” Owens said.

As Stewart and Owens rode north, out of town, they neither saw, nor were seen by Lucas Cain, who was just approaching from the south.

Lucas took Charley II to the livery to be fed and curried. The stable keeper was an older man with white hair and a white beard. When he approached Charley II, he did so gently, rubbing the horse’s nose and working his hand behind Charley II’s ears.

“I want him fed and curried,” Lucas said.

“Will you be boarding this fine looking horse for the night?”

“I’ll pay for the night whether I stay or not,” Lucas said. “It depends on what I find out while I’m in town.”

“What you find out? What sort of information are you looking for?”

“I’m looking for some men, not quite sure how many, but one of them, their leader, has a bad eye.”

“Yeah, they was here. There was three of ‘em, but two of ‘em has rode away.” The liveryman pointed to star-faced gelding. “That’s the horse of the one that’s still here. I don’t know his name, don’t know none of ‘em’s names, but I know what they all look like. There was the one fella with the bad eye like you was sayin'. One of 'em had sort of a hook nose 'n a chin that stuck out so's you'd think they're about to touch together. One of 'em is a runty lookin' little bastard 'n that's the one that's still here."

"Yeah, the men I'm looking for. Thanks, you've been a big help," Lucas said, giving the man a five dollar bill.

27

Lucas wondered why Bundy was left behind, but he decided it was probably a good thing. It would be an easier task to confront them one at a time. Leaving the stable, he crossed the street to the Horseshoe Saloon. When he went inside he saw the bartender was at the far end of the bar. He picked up a couple of whiskey glasses, each with about an inch of whiskey remaining. The bartender shrugged his shoulders, then removed the cap from the bottle, and returned the whiskey to its original container.

"Whiskey," Lucas said.

The bartender looked down toward Lucas, and saw a tall man with broad shoulders. But it was the cold, blue eyes that caught his attention. That, and the Colt pistol at his side, which was worn in the way of a man who knows how to use it. The bartender knew about such men, and he was afraid this man meant trouble. The bartender stared at him, totally forgetting that his job was to tend bar.

"I said whiskey," Lucas repeated in the same, deep voice as before.

"Oh, uh, yes, of course," the bartender replied. He started to pour the whiskey from the same bottle into which he had just emptied the two glasses.

"From a new bottle."

"All right." The bartender picked up a new bottle, but his hand was shaking so that it looked as if he might spill it.

"Here, let me do it," Lucas offered, taking the bottle from the bartender. He poured himself a glass of whiskey, returned the bottle, then lay a quarter on the bar.

"My name is Lucas Cain, and I'm looking for a man who may be in here."

Someone heard Lucas give his name, and he passed it on to another, then the name circled through the room until everyone was aware that he was here. And there were very few who had never heard of him.

"Who, uh—" The bartender paused, and cleared his throat before he could speak again. "Who are you looking for?"

"A little runt of a man who rides with Dudley Stewart."

The bartender said nothing, but he looked to the head of the stairs, where earlier, he had seen Bundy take Aggie.

"I see," Lucas said, smiling easily. "He's upstairs."

"I didn't say anything about him being upstairs," the bartender replied, quickly.

"You didn't have to."

"What do you want with him?"

"Hmm, I assumed that when you heard my name, you would know what I wanted with him. I intend to turn him over to the nearest sheriff, alive if that's possible, but dead if that's needed."

Lucas said the words quietly, but as had his name earlier, his stated intention spread quickly around the room, and conversations stopped and card games were halted as the promise of drama manifested itself.

"What did you just say, Mister?" someone asked.

Lucas looked toward the man who had just asked the question. He was tall and thin, with white hair and a bushy white moustache. He was wearing a star penned to his shirt.

"You must be the sheriff."

"That I am, and I've no intention of allowing any cold-blooded killing take place in my town." The sheriff spoke nervously.

"I appreciate that, Sheriff, and I respect your position on this. I have no intention of killing him without justification. As a deputy U.S. Marshal, it is my intention to arrest him, but if he refuses to come along peacefully, if he goes for his gun, I'll have no choice but to defend myself."

The sheriff addressed the others in the room. "You heard what Mr. Cain said. He intends to brace the man fair and square, 'n I intend to let him do just that. But, if he ain't on the up 'n up, then I'll do what I can to either stop it or hold Cain accountable."

"That there's the way it ought to be done," one of the saloon patrons said, to the agreement of the others.

Lucas nodded, and turned back toward the bar. The piano player who had stopped for the discourse returned to his piano to resume playing, however, all eyes were on the top of the stairs, and all conversation directed toward the upcoming gunfight. Within a moment the piano stopped playing again, and everyone grew silent as they looked toward the head of the stairs, and waited.

The waiting grew more strained, and the conversation soon petered out. Now there was absolute silence, and when someone coughed, everyone turned to look at him accusingly. The clock on the wall ticked loudly as the pendulum swung back and forth in measured movements. Involuntarily, half a dozen or more men looked up at the clock, as if it were very important to fix the time, the better to be able to tell the story later.

The whiskey glasses were filled as quietly as everything else, with the men walking silently over to the bar, then holding them out so they could be refilled without a word being spoken.

More customers came into the saloon, but they were met at the door with whispered conversations as to what was going on. As a result, they wandered wordlessly up to the bar, and had their glass filled as silently as the other patrons.

They all waited.

The tension grew almost unbearable. From the room at the top of the stairs, came the sound of a woman's moan of passion, a little too loud to be real, but convincing, never the less. There wasn't a man present who didn't know what was going on up there, but what would have normally brought embarrassed laughter, now brought only silence.

The man upstairs said something, his voice a low, unintelligible rumble, and it was answered by a peal of forced laughter. There was the sound of footfalls as boots struck the floor, and the man and woman came out of the room, talking and laughing.

They started down the stairs before they noticed the deathly silence and everyone staring up at them.

"Honey, what is this? What's going on?" Aggie said, her voice strained with fright.

"I think maybe you'd better go back upstairs," Bundy said. Aggie responded and scurried back up the stairs, out of the way.

"Hello, Mister, my name is Lucas Cain, and I've been looking for you and the others."

Bundy glanced hurriedly around the room.

"Oh, if you're looking for the others, I'm afraid they've gone on without you. I have no idea where that might be, though. Perhaps you can tell me."

"I'll be damn. Those dirty bastards ran out on me," Bundy said. "I guess you know what they say. There's no honor among thieves."

"That said, would you like to tell me where they went?"

"I think not."

"This man is the sheriff here," Lucas said, pointing to the man with the star. "If you'll give yourself up, I'll turn you over to him. You're worth as much to me alive as you are dead. I'm perfectly willing to take you in alive."

Bundy smiled. "Now, what good would that do me? You know damn well that once I'm in the hands of the law, they're going to hang old Pete Bundy." He shook his head. "I can't give myself up."

"Don't do it, Pete."

Even as Lucas issued his warning, Bundy's hand dipped to his holstered gun and he pulled it free. But Lucas had his gun out in a blur, pulling the trigger as the gun came to bear, sending a bullet into Bundy's chest. Bundy was unable to get a shot off and he fell against the wall, then slid the rest of the way down the stairs, face down.

Lucas hurried over to him, then turned him over. Bundy opened his eyes and looked up at Lucas.

"Damn," he said. "Damn, if I had known it was going to hurt this much, I would have gone back and let 'em hang me."

"The rope might hurt more," Lucas said.

"Yeah, you might be right," Bundy said, grunting the words, painfully. "So, Stewart and Owens left me, did they?"

"It would appear so."

"The sons of bitches," Coker said.

"You think you could drink a little whiskey?" Lucas said. "It might dull the pain of dying a bit."

"Yeah, get me some whiskey," Bundy said, his voice showing the pain he was in.

Lucas walked over the bar, got a bottle of whiskey, then returned to the man who was lying on the floor, the center of attention to everyone in the saloon. He raised Bundy up far enough so he could drink, then gave him the bottle. Bundy took several long swallows.

"Pecos," Bundy said.

"What?"

"You'll find Dudley Stewart and Herman Owens in Pecos, the sons of bitches."

"Thanks."

"The whiskey didn't help much. Damn it hurts."

Those were his last words. He gasped a couple of times, then he was gone.

28

When Lucas got back to the livery, the stableman was standing in the door.

"Did you feed my horse?" Lucas asked.

"Yep. Rubbed him down, too."

"That's good, he's goin' to need it." Lucas took his saddle down from the top of the stall, then threw it across Charley II's back.

"I heard shootin' over in the saloon," the stableman said. "Was that you?"

"It was."

"Yeah, well, I sort of figured it was. 'N since you're alive, I'm goin' to figure the other feller's dead."

"That's right."

"So, that means there's two of 'em left. You'll be goin' after 'em, I reckon."

Lucas finished the job of saddling Charley II, then led him over to the watering trough.

"They're in Pecos."

"That's about five miles from here," the liveryman said.

When Charley II had drunk his fill, he raised his head up from the trough with water still dripping from his lips. Lucas swung into the saddle.

"Just about as far as a horse can go at a gallop," Lucas said.

"You plannin' on runnin' 'im all the way?"

"I've got to. Now that I'm this close, I'm not planning on letting those two get away from me."

Lucas trotted until they were out of town, then he slapped his legs at the animal's side, and Charley II broke into a gallop. Lucas settled back into the saddle matching the horse's rhythm with his own. He could feel the wind in his face, and hear the drumming of hoofbeats as Charley II kicked up little puffs of dust behind them. He let himself flow into the horse so that for the duration of the run, it was as if he and Charley II were sharing the same muscle structure and bloodstream.

As he rode, Lucas thought of the task before him. This was the day of reckoning for Dudley Stewart. Of that, he had no doubt.

As Lucas galloped toward them, Stewart and Owens stepped into the bank in Pecos.

There was one customer, standing at the teller's cage.

"Get your hands up," Stewart ordered.

"Here, what is this?" the teller asked.

"It's a bank robbery," Stewart said, waving his pistol. "What does it look like? You," he said to the teller, "stand over against that wall where I can see you. If you move, my friend here, will kill you."

"No, don't shoot, don't shoot, I'll do as you say," the

bank customer, a thin, bald-headed man who was wearing glasses replied.

"The bank manager here?" Stewart asked the teller.

"Yes, that would be Mr. Hiram Dempster. He's in his office."

"Get him out here."

"Yes, sir, yes, sir."

The teller disappeared, and a moment later returned with the bank manager. He was a very dignified looking man, well dressed, with a well-kempt moustache and streaks of silver in his hair.

"What's going on here?" Dempster said importantly. "What is the meaning of this?"

"What does it look like? I'm robbing the bank."

"See here, you can't do that. People have their money in this bank."

Stewart raised his pistol. "This says I can do it. You," he said, pointing the pistol toward the teller. "Go open the safe and start taking the money out."

"What shall I do, Mr. Dempster?"

"You had better do as he says, Mr. Lewis," Dempster replied.

"You have one of those cloth bags you use to move money around?" Stewart asked.

"Uh, no, I don't think so," Dempster said.

"That's all right. Take off your long-handle underwear."

"What?" Dempster asked.

"Lewis can tie a knot in one of the legs, and fill it with money."

"I, uh, think we might have a transfer bag, now that I think of it," Dempster said. "Mr. Lewis, start putting money in a transfer bag just as he says."

Lewis got a bag from under the counter, then he

opened the safe and began taking out money and dropping it into the bag.

"Hurry up," Stewart said.

"I-I'm going as fast as I can," Lewis said.

"Take a look outside," Stewart said to Owens. "See what's going on out there."

"There's a woman coming into the bank," Owens said.

"Grab her when she comes in."

"No, that's my wife!" Dempster said, glancing through the window. "Please don't hurt her!"

"Yeah, well, she should 'a had better sense than to come into the bank when it was being robbed," Stewart said with an evil laugh.

The door opened, and a middle-aged, rather attractive woman came in.

"Hiram, I need—" she started to say, then she saw her husband and another standing near the wall with their arms raised. Mr. Lewis was shuffling money into a bag.

"Oh, my God! You're robbing the bank!"

"Marilou, run!" Dempster shouted.

Marilou turned toward the door.

"Stop her," Stewart said.

Owens reached out, grabbed the woman by her arm, and jerked her back away from the door.

"You ain't goin' nowhere, lady!" Owens said in a growling voice.

Marilou screamed.

"Shut her up!" Stewart ordered.

Owens slapped the woman hard, and as he did so, Lewis, taking advantage of the disturbance, dropped the half-full bag of money, and made a run toward the back door of the bank.

Stewart, seeing him run, shot at him just as he

opened the back door. Lewis pitched forward into the alley, bleeding from the bullet hole in the back of his head.

"You...you killed him!" Dempster said in a shocked tone of voice.

"Yeah," Stewart grunted. "I reckon I did."

"HEY, EVER' body! Somethin's goin' on in the bank," someone from the street shouted. "I heard a gunshot!"

"The bank's bein' robbed!" another shouted.

"Stewart, they found out we're in here," Owens shouted. "They're gatherin' up. Damn if it don't look like they're a' plannin' on comin' in here. What'll we do?"

Holding his gun on the bank president, his wife, and the bank customer, Stewart eased over to the window to have a look outside. He could see the townspeople scurrying about, gathering guns and putting up barricades.

"We ain't a' goin' to make it out of here, Stewart. They'll shoot us down in the street."

"You should have thought of that before you came in here," Dempster said. "There are a lot of good and courageous people in Pecos. You'd better give yourselves up. That's the only way you're going to get out of here alive."

Stewart stroked his chin, spending a long moment thinking over the situation. Then, he smiled a broad, evil smile.

"No, it ain't the only thing we can do. We're goin' to make it out of here," he said.

"How are we going to do that, Stewart? There's only two of us, and the whole town's out there."

"Wrong, Mr. Owens. There will be three of us going out the door."

"Three of us?"

"You, me, and the woman." He pointed toward the bank president's wife. "What was your name again? Oh, yes, it was Marilou, I believe. Go pick up the moneybag, Marilou. We'll be going out the front door."

"What are you going out the front door for? Our horses is in the back."

"Yes, but we ain't leaving on horses, we're leavin' town in style."

"Please, don't take my wife. Take me," Dempster pleaded.

"Hell, what good would it do to take you? You're a banker, nobody would hold their fire because of you. Half the town would probably like to see you dead anyway. No, we'll be takin' the woman."

"You won't get away with this, you know," Dempster said to Stewart.

"Oh, I think we will. And you're going to help us."

"Why would I help you? I have an obligation to my depositors."

"Because if you don't help us, I'm goin' to kill your wife."

Marilou gasped.

"No, no, please—what do you want me to do?"

"I want you to go outside 'n let them people know that we got Marilou, 'n if any of 'em starts shootin', we'll kill her."

"No, I won't do that," the banker said.

"Hiram, for God's sake, do what they say!" Marilou said, her voice pitched high with fear.

"All right, all right," the banker agreed.

Dempster stepped outside and held his hands up in the air. "They're comin' out!" he shouted. "They've got my wife with them, so for God's sake, don't anyone shoot."

A moment later two men and Marilou Dempster came out of the bank. One of the two men was carrying a canvas bag that everyone knew must be full of money. The other man was holding his gun to the woman's temple. Everyone watched as they walked down to the stage depot.

LUCAS HAD HELD Charley II to a gallop for much of the way, but he slowed him to a trot for the last five minutes, then to a walk as he came into the town of Pecos.

As he arrived in town, he saw a large crowd of people in the middle of the street. They were obviously agitated about something, and Lucas was certain he knew what it was. He swung down from the saddle in front of the sheriff's office. He tied his now sweating horse off at the hitching rail, then used his hat to brush away some of the dust that the ride had generated.

The deputy was standing at the window, looking out into the street. He glanced around when Lucas came into the office.

"Somethin' I can do for you, mister?" The deputy was a young man, in his early to mid-twenties, and he was drinking coffee. He took a sip, then examined Lucas over the rim of his cup.

"I'd like to see the sheriff," Lucas replied.

"Yeah? Well, in case you ain't noticed, mister, we got us some sort of a situation goin' here."

"You just had your bank robbed," Lucas said. It was a declarative statement, not a question.

The cup was halfway to the deputy's lips when he stopped, then brought it back down and stared at Lucas suspiciously.

"Yeah," he said, "the bank was just robbed. How is it that you know about it?"

"I can also tell you who did it. It's Dudley Stewart and Herman Owens."

"How do you know that, Mister…who the hell are you, anyway?"

"I am Marshal Lucas Cain. Now please tell me where I can find the sheriff."

The deputy's expression of suspicion was replaced by one of awe and trepidation.

"Su…uh…sure thing, Marshal. He's out in the street, standin' over there in front of the general store. He's the tall, skinny fella. Uh, is this something important?"

"Look at my horse, Deputy? Do you think I would ride him like that if this wasn't important?"

"No, sir, I don't guess you would."

Lucas picked his way through the crowd until he reached the sheriff. The sheriff was surrounded by half a dozen of the townsmen.

"You've got to do something, Sheriff. My wife is in there," a well-dressed man was saying.

"Well now, Hiram, just what is it that you want me to do?" the sheriff asked.

"I want you to get my wife away from those men."

Suddenly some shots rang out down at the stage depot. Hearing that, the people in the street began to scatter; a few of the women screamed, and some of the men called out in fear.

"Get off the street!" the sheriff shouted, waving the people aside. "Ever'one, get off the street!"

Men and women ran in between the buildings, and dived down behind the porches and watering troughs. Several ran inside some of the businesses.

The sheriff stepped up onto the porch in front of the general store. He and several others were staring at the depot, which was at the far end of Main Street.

"That was real smart of you, Sheriff," Stewart shouted "You tell ever'one to keep their distance, 'n none of 'em will get hurt."

"What do you want?"

"I'm going to send someone down to talk to you. He'll tell you what I want."

The door to the stage depot opened, and someone stepped out onto the depot porch. He was holding his hands up.

"Sheriff, there's somebody comin'," someone said.

The man with his hands up started toward them. "Don't shoot, don't shoot, please, don't anyone shoot! It's me, Abe Dooley!"

"It's Abe Dooley," someone said, as if Dooley hadn't already identified himself.

"It's me, Abe Dooley, the ticket agent," he said again. He was moving slowly down the street toward the sheriff, holding both arms high in the air.

"Come ahead, Abe," the sheriff said.

"Don't shoot!" Dooley called.

"Damnit, Abe, do you really think someone is going to shoot you? Now, come on over here. And put your hands down. You look ridiculous."

Walking slowly, and obviously very frightened, Dooley moved down to the middle of the town, all the while keeping his hands up.

"Put your hands down, Abe. You're not our prisoner."

"Thank God," Dooley said as he lowered his hands. "Thank God I'm out of there."

"How many are in there?" Lucas asked.

The sheriff looked around, noticing Lucas for the first time. "Who the hell are you?" he asked."I'm Marshal Lucas Cain. I've been trailing Stewart and Owens for some time now. And unless I miss my guess, I've just caught up with them."

"I don't know if that's who's in there or not. But whoever it is, it ain't your problem, it's mine."

"Wrong, Sheriff," Lucas replied, coldly. "I've been chasing those two men for a long time. I'm not about to walk away from them now."

"Lucas Cain, you say? Yeah, I've heard of you."

Lucas didn't answer.

"Well, Marshal Cain, we don't even know if that's who we've got in there. So why don't you just back away, and let me take care of my business?"

"That's who's in there, all right, Sheriff," Dooley said. "Dudley Stewart and Herman Owens. And they done seen you, too, Marshal. They want you to come in there. They said they want to talk to you."

"That's all they want? To talk to Cain?"

"Yeah, that and a stagecoach."

"What? They want a ticket on the stagecoach?"

"Not exactly...they want the coach. They want any passengers that might be on it to get off here, so they are the only ones on the coach. They plan to take Mrs. Dempster with them, and they say they'll let her off safely about five miles down the road."

"Do it, Sheriff, for God's sake, do it," Dempster pleaded.

"What about the passengers who might leave from here?"

"There were only two of them, Chris Yancey and his wife."

"Did you say, 'were' only two?"

"Yeah, did you hear the shooting a few minutes ago? They killed Chris and his wife."

There were gasps of shock and sorrow from those who were gathered around the sheriff.

"What about Cain?"

Dooley cleared his throat, and looked at the ground.

"What did they say about Cain?" the sheriff asked again.

"They, uh, they said they had other plans for him."

"I'll just bet they do," Lucas said, chuckling. He stepped down from the porch and started walking toward the stage depot.

"Here!" the sheriff called. "Cain, just where do you think you're going?"

"I'm going to talk to them. That's what they said they wanted, isn't it?"

"I can't let you do that. This is none of your affair."

"Let him go!" Dempster pleaded. "He said he's a U.S. Marshal, didn't he? He's probably got a lot of experience dealing with people like this."

"No," the sheriff insisted. "Cain, you get back here, right now. I am not going to let you go down there."

"Sheriff, shoot me in the back, or shut the hell up," Lucas said as he continued his march toward the stage depot.

Lucas could feel all eyes on him as he continued his walk down the dusty street. When he reached the depot, he stepped up onto the platform, then went inside the building. In contrast to the bright sunshine outside, the interior of the building was in dark shadow.

"Well now, lookie here who come in, Owens," Stewart said. "I didn't figure he would accept our invitation."

Stewart was in the middle of the floor next to an iron stove. It had been sometime since the stove had been used last, but the tang of burnt wood hung around it still.

The woman, her eyes open wide in terror, was standing next to Stewart. Stewart was holding his pistol to her temple. Owens was standing at the window, keeping an eye on the street.

"I thought you was supposed to be a smart man, Cain, but here you are," Owens said. "Yes, sir, here you are, and there's nothing you can do about it. That was really dumb."

"Isn't this what you asked me to do?"

"Well, hell, if we knowed it was that easy, we would've asked you a long time ago to just come waltzin' to us, so's we could shoot you."

"Oh, you mean that's what you have in mind?" Lucas's voice was calm and conversational.

"Yeah. What did you think we wanted?" Stewart asked.

"I don't know, I sort of thought you two might be wanting to give yourselves up and let me take you in."

"What?" Stewart shouted. He began laughing. "You hear that, Owens? This dumb son of a bitch thought we wanted to give ourselves up." He laughed again, this time joined in laughter by Owens.

"You may as well let the woman go, Stewart," Lucas said. "She won't do you any good."

"The hell she won't. She's our ticket out of here."

"No, she's not."

"What the hell do you mean she's not?" Stewart demanded, the tone of his voice showing frustration.

"I mean I'm not letting you leave with or without her."

"You're out of your mind. What you don't understand is, I don't care whether I kill this woman or not."

"No, *you* don't understand," Lucas replied. "This woman is nothing to me, so I don't care whether or not you kill her. Because either way, I'm going to kill you."

"What? Don't you see I've got this gun pointed at this woman's head?"

"Yeah, and therein lies your problem," Lucas said. "You see, you have your gun pointed at her, not at me. And while you're killing her, I'll be killing you."

Lucas started his draw, and Stewart realized that killing the woman wouldn't save him, and his only chance would be to turn the gun toward Lucas. But it was too late. Even as he was pulling the gun away from the woman, Lucas was pulling the trigger. Stewart didn't even get a shot off.

Marilou let out a little shout of fear as the bullet hit Stewart right between the eyes, and some of the blood splashed onto her.

It all happened too fast for Owens. He was so sure that the threat of killing the banker's wife would stop Cain that he had made no attempt to defend himself. But when he saw Stewart go down, he jerked his gun away from the window. Unlike Stewart, who died with his gun unfired, Owens did manage to get off a shot, but his bullet poked a hole in the floor.

"SHERIFF, SOMEONE'S COMIN'," somebody called.

"Hold your fire, it's Cain, and he has Mrs. Dempster!"

When they saw Cain and Mrs. Dempster leave the

stage coach depot, the townspeople began moving cautiously toward them.

"Marilou! Marilou! Are you all right?" Dempster shouted.

"Hiram! Hiram!" Marilou said, as she broke into a run toward her husband.

Dempster met her halfway, and several of the townspeople as well.

"I believe this belongs to your bank," Lucas said, handing the moneybag over to Dempster.

"Thanks," Dempster said. Then, turning back to his wife, he saw blood on her face. "You're bleeding!" Dempster said. "Marilou, are you hurt?"

"No, this is Stewart's blood. He was holding me when Mr. Cain shot him."

"My God, man!" the sheriff said. "You shot it out with him when he was holding Mrs. Dempster that close? What's wrong with you? Don't you care about anyone's life? Just who the hell do you think you are?"

"Sheriff, listen to yourself," Marilou said. "Why are you shouting at him like that? Don't you realize that this man saved my life?"

"Yes, but he...he—"

"He what?" Marilou asked.

The sheriff looked at Lucas for a long moment, obviously trying to hold off the anger that had seized him. Finally, he knew that he was wrong, and he sighed.

"I guess I do owe you my thanks," the sheriff said. He took in the crowd with a wave of his hand. "In fact, we all owe you our thanks."

"Keep your thanks, Sheriff. There are four corpses lying on the floor back there, and two of them are Stewart and Owens. I believe there's paper on both of them. That's all I want."

Lucas stayed in Pecos, just long enough to collect his reward. Then, with the money in his pocket, and as yet no known outlaw to pursue, he left town with the idea that he would retrieve the body of Sam Coker. Then he would head out with no particular destination in mind.

Once again, Lucas Cain was a rambling man.

A LOOK AT: ROBERT VAUGHAN'S THE CHANEY BROTHERS WESTERN ADVENTURES

THE COMPLETE SERIES

***New York Times* bestselling author Robert Vaughan's classic masterpiece series combining epic adventure and the search for truth and justice in an oftentimes lawless land, available for the first time complete and unabridged.**

Once they fought on opposite sides of a war. Now they're fighting for justice and revenge!

They Came from one Missouri family, but Lance and Buck Chaney had been fighting on opposite sides of the war—until they were brought together by a shipment of gold dust. Fighting for the Confederacy, Buck had been ordered to hijack the gold his brother's Union troops were bringing north to Jefferson City. By the time the skirmish was over the shipment of gold was missing. Now the former enemies have joined together again—to hunt down the man who had taken the gold from them both in an act of treachery and bloodshed.

It Takes Two Loyal Brothers to Outsmart a Texas Outlaw.

Buck Chaney first crosses paths with Rufus Blanton on a West Texas train car halted suddenly in the night. Rufus is on board-and set on robbing every passenger. When a shootout with Buck leaves two of his gunmen dead, the outlaw gets away with his life - but without any loot. He'll come back to haunt Buck Chaney and his brother Lance.

When Lance Chaney's ex-commanding officer from the Civil War comes to him for help, the Barlow Marshal cannot refuse, even when things don't add up.

With his brother Buck riding alongside him, the pair find more trouble than they care to. From Indians, to outlaws, their trail is dotted with violence.

Meanwhile back in Barlow, Lance's remaining deputy is killed, leaving the town wide open for the lawless. But out of the freezing winter comes a one-eyed man who seems to be fit for the job.

Except Ben Travers has a plan. He and his gang are going to take Barlow for all it has, and he doesn't care how many corpses he has to walk over to get it.

After being seriously wounded in his pursuit of the Carter brothers, Deputy Marshal Buck Chaney wakes to find himself in the middle of a sheep war in Blanco County, Texas.

On one side are the Texas cattlemen who'll do whatever it takes to rid the range of the animals and those who come with them. On the other is a Mexican family who only wanted to be left alone. Outgunned, Buck sends for help from his brother.

But Lance Chaney has problems of his own.

The newly appointed sheriff of Comanche County has a killer in his town who is hellbent on blotting out something from his past and wants no remaining witnesses. The corpses stack up until the main suspect is murdered in jail, with his dying breath he utters the words, "Grand Valley."

Now Lance must dig into the past to find a killer before it's too late.

Two brothers, counties apart, and fighting a stacked deck. In the end it's only the law that counts. Their law. Chaney Law...

***Robert Vaughan's The Chaney Brothers Western Adventures: The Complete and Unabridged Series* contains the following titles:**

GLORY DUST

THE CHANEY EDGE

THE HUNTERS

CHANEY LAW

AVAILABLE NOW

ABOUT THE AUTHOR

Robert Vaughan sold his first book when he was 19. That was 57 years and nearly 500 books ago. He wrote the novelization for the miniseries *Andersonville*. Vaughan wrote, produced, and appeared in the History Channel documentary *Vietnam Homecoming*. His books have hit the NYT bestseller list seven times. He has won the Spur Award, the PORGIE Award (Best Paperback Original), the Western Fictioneers Lifetime Achievement Award, received the Readwest President's Award for Excellence in Western Fiction, is a member of the American Writers Hall of Fame and is a Pulitzer Prize nominee. Vaughn is also a retired army officer, helicopter pilot with three tours in Vietnam. And received the Distinguished Flying Cross, the Purple Heart, The Bronze Star with three oak leaf clusters, the Air Medal for valor with 35 oak leaf clusters, the Army Commendation Medal, the Meritorious Service Medal, and the Vietnamese Cross of Gallantry.

Made in United States
Troutdale, OR
02/24/2024